Craved by a Beast

Phoenix Pack Urban Paranormal Book 2

JADE ROYAL

Other Works by Jade Royal

- Love is Worth the Sacrifice (Completed Series)
- Two Halves of a Broken Heart
- How Deep is Your Love (Completed Series)
- Saved by a Beast (Phoenix Pack Paranormal Series)

© **2018**

Published by *Miss Candice Presents*

Prologue

Jayce looked up from the small piece of wood he was carving when he heard commotion just outside of his small cabin. He lived alone once he matured into puberty and his parents retired to another pack. They were both submissive wolves who couldn't 0really take the heat of an active pack with too many dominant wolves. Jayce himself was always an anomaly because he was a dominant wolf born from two submissive wolves, and since he was a pup, he learned that he was going to end up losing his parents to another pack because they couldn't deal with the dominant vibes, but with friends like Jaxson, Kellan, and Tristan, Jayce was able to still feel like he had family in the pack once his parents left.

Getting up from where he was, he looked out of his front window and could see his pack members walking towards the middle of their territory where they always often gathered. There was a buzz in the air as the wolves chatted about whatever was going on. A sharp rapping sound came at his door. He moved from the window and went to answer the door. His friends were waiting outside for him.

"What's going on?" Jayce asked.

"A lone wolf came wandering into the territory. My father's trying to deal with her now. No one knows if she's rogue or not, she's not saying anything, and she won't shift," Kellan informed him. Jayce left his place and followed his friends to where all the commotion was happening. The entire pack was gathered looking on as their alpha was trying to talk to the omega. Obviously, a female because of her size, she was in her wolf form. Jayce didn't remember ever seeing a wolf-like hers before. Her fur was a deep cinnamon with gold flecks, and her eyes were a fierce glaze of toffee. Jayce's wolf snapped his head up noticing the rogue wolf immediately. Jayce felt himself pushing his friends out of his way as he got closer.

"Watch yourself." Tristan warned, but Jayce couldn't hear anything else that was going on. It was like he was in a trance and couldn't stop walking towards the wolf. He parted the crowd of his pack mates. When he broke the edge of the crowd, the she-wolf looked at him immediately.

Tell your alpha to back off. I didn't know this was pack territory. I want to leave, her melodic voice rang in his head. She spoke in a calm tone, but he smelled her anxiety and her fear of Kameron.

Why don't you tell him? Jayce asked her. She growled at him for everyone to hear, including the alpha. Kameron turned and looked at Jayce.

"Do you know her?" Kameron asked him urgently.

"No," Jayce replied. "She just told me to tell you to back off. She didn't know a pack lived here, and she wants to leave. I told her to tell you herself, and that's why she's growling at me."

"Well, ask her why the hell she's not talking to me." Kameron gritted.

Why does he think? I'm a goddamn omega, and he's overpowering me with his alpha vibes. Like, damn, I know he's the alpha already. He can tone that shit down now. Does he expect me to be forthcoming? she said to Jayce. Jayce actually couldn't help but smile. Her attitude appealed to him. Jayce chuckled and looked at his alpha.

"Your vibes are overpowering her," Jayce informed him.

"Basically, she's saying you're too intimidating." The wolf effectively backed up when Kameron looked at her again. The wolf looked at Jayce and sniffed the air. Her tail began to wag happily. Jayce's wolf pushed at him trying to get free to meet the wolf personally , but Jayce kept him inside. His wolf wanted to meet her, but Jayce wanted to meet her human.

"Can I?" Jayce asked his alpha. Kameron backed away and allowed Jayce to get close to the wolf. He didn't think Jayce would succeed, but he ended up kneeled in front of the omega.

"Your wolf is beautiful," Jayce whispered to her, running his hand through her fur. She licked his face and wagged her tail harder.

Stop flirting with my animal, she said.

"Well, if you shifted back, then maybe I can flirt with you."

Is your alpha going to harm me? I know packs don't like omegas, but I'm not trying to steal food or ruin your pack grounds.

"No one will hurt you. Trust me." In a flash of power, the wolf shimmered, and out emerged a cocoa colored beauty with long sister locks, and cinnamon colored eyes. A burst of pomegranate, blackberries, and spice smacked him across his senses. He felt his wolf eyes glow as she emerged from her wolf. She curled up trying to cover her naked body. Jayce reached out to her and pulled her into his lap. She breathed in deep. Spearmint and something citrus hit her. Her wolf eyes began to glow. They looked at each other with glowing eyes.

"Mine." He growled lowly.

"Mine." She breathed feeling the connection of a mating call. He touched her locks and moved down to her face and ran a thumb over her silky lips. She smiled when he poked at her septum piercing.

"Jayce," Kameron said. Jayce blinked from the small trance he had with his mate. Jayce began to stand and put the omega behind him to cover her nakedness from the eyes of the pack. She stuck her head out from behind Jayce.

"Who are you?" Kameron asked her.

"Rita," she replied. "I've been without a pack for years now. I was just looking for food, and I smelled wolves, so I came to see who was here." Kameron looked at the way Jayce shielded her.

"Our rules forbid us to allow omegas into the pack without extensive research of their backgrounds, or to even allow them on our grounds, but I'm asking you, Kameron, to make an exception this time."

"And why is that?" Kameron asked crossing his arms. Jayce looked at Rita.

"Seems like the little omega is my mate." Jayce revealed. He looked over to his friends who wore shock filled expressions, and then Kellan held his hand out for Tristan and Jaxson who slapped money into it.

"I'll get my money from you later," Kellan said to Jayce. Jayce rolled his eyes. They all had a bet that Kellan would be the first to find his mate, but Kellan insisted it wouldn't be him. Jayce never thought he'd be the first, and now obviously, he was dead wrong.

****

Rita watched as her mate came from the woods, trotting like he didn't have a care in the world. His friends were with him, and they were talking amongst each other. Rita sensed the bond they had the moment she began to feel her mate's emotions. She'd been inducted into Kameron's pack over a month ago, and this was her new home but when it came to her mate, she was unsure where she stood, but all his friends had accepted her with no problem.

"What's up, Ri?" Jaxson asked as they approached her.

"Nothing," she replied. Without Jayce and his friends, Rita didn't have friends in the pack. Being the newcomer, it was going to take the wolves a while to trust her, especially since she was an omega, to begin with.

"You should try talking with the other wolves," Kellan said. As the son of the alpha pair, Rita felt his alpha vibes, but he never exuded it purposely. He was just a strong wolf meant to be the leader of a pack. Her wolf respected him, and he looked out for her.

"I do." Rita sighed.

"They pretty much give me weird glances and short answers before moving on."

"Your mate is the beta of the pack. It's an important role. I'm pretty sure he can make it, so the pack members befriend you."

"I can do that," Jayce said.

"But I don't see the point in it. Rita wants genuine friends, not people who were forced to befriend her." Rita nodded agreeing with what her mate said. She felt her arousal but stomped it out quickly. He hadn't made a sexual gesture to her, so Rita didn't want to make one towards him first.

"Don't worry about it then," Jaxson said. He slung his arm around Rita's shoulders.

"I'll be your friend." He pulled at one of her locks making her smile, but Jayce growled.

"Pipe down, wolfie, I know she's all yours. Doesn't mean I can't be her bestie." Jaxson liked to rile his friends up, and just because he wanted to get a reaction out of Jayce, he leaned over and gave Rita a healthy kiss on her cheek, making sure to make it a loud smack. Jayce bared his canines and roared. Jaxson snickered before taking off as Jayce chased him.

"I guess I better go break it up," Tristan said.

"No doubt they're gonna end up rolling around on the ground trading punches." He took off following Jayce and Jaxson leaving Rita and Kellan standing there.

"Men," Rita said shaking her head.

"Mated men, you mean," Kellan said. He was smiling until it disappeared suddenly.

"I gotta take off. My parents wanna talk to me."

"Are you going to be the next alpha?" Rita asked him. Kellan shrugged.

"Depends. As you can tell, I'm not the iron fist alpha like my father, but no worries, as long as you're with Jayce, you'll be protected."

"My wolf likes you," she said.

"You make her feel calm. Kameron...he's a good alpha, but he makes her nervous."

"Don't take it personal. That's just his natural vibe." Kellan smiled. He rubbed her shoulder before starting to walk off.

By nightfall, Rita was alone sitting under the stars while everyone else had retired to their cabins or caves. Kameron had set her up with a small cabin, but she secretly wished Jayce had invited her to stay with him. Since he didn't, she gave him as much space as he needed. After he ran after Jaxson, he hadn't returned to her. She figured he was doing his Beta duties. Even still, Rita longed for him, especially since she was alone, to begin with. Now, she'd found her mate, and everything she felt she was missing out on life with, she was able to get it back. No wonder her wolf kept telling her to come in this direction in the first place. Rita never went on pack territories, but this one, her wolf wouldn't let her walk by.

"Is that longing I smell, with a little bit of arousal?" Rita jumped at the strange voice. The shifter was standing in her space, hovering above her.

"Back off," she said immediately. She didn't have time to deal with wolves and their hormones.

"Come on, sugar. Give me a shot." He sniffed at her.

"You're not claimed. I don't see a mark or smell a male on you."

"That doesn't give you the right to be all up in my face." She stood ready to walk off, but he darted in front of her not wanting her to leave.

"Look, Omega, you should be happy as fuck I'm even paying you any attention, so quit the hard to get act and let me lay it on you." Rita unsheathed her claws seeing that he wasn't going to let her walk off without a fight. He reached forward to grab onto her, but his hand stopped mid-motion. Jayce had him by the wrist, digging his claws into the male's wrist, drawing blood.

"Correct me if I'm wrong, but I swore you were about to put your dusty ass hand on my mate."

"Mate?" The wolf babbled.

"I didn't-I didn't know she belonged to anyone."

"Are you challenging me?"

"What? No! I would never challenge the Beta."

"Touching the mate of any wolf is a sign of a challenge."

"I didn't know she was your mate, Jayce! She doesn't carry your scent! I promise it won't happen again."

"Ya' damn straight it won't happen again." Jayce easily twisted the wolf's wrist until it snapped and then twisted his arm from the socket.

"Healing should keep you busy for a couple of days. Touch my mate again, and I'll break more than your arm." Crying out in pain, the wolf scampered off whimpering. Jayce inhaled and looked at Rita. Her amazing scent was as vibrant as ever, but the faint smell of honey was dripping from her insides. She was getting aroused.

"Let's go," he stated, turning and walking off. Rita was stuck for a moment until he turned and looked at her. She snapped from her trance and followed him all the way to his cabin.

Inside, Rita stood by the door hugging herself. She'd been in his cabin before. After they realized they were mates, he brought her to his place and cooked dinner for her, and they talked all night, and then on other occasions during the week, she would visit him, but she never stayed the night.

"Did you eat something?" he asked her as he pulled the t-shirt he was wearing over his head and off.

"Ye-yeah." She stumbled as she looked at his body longingly. He continued to the back of the cabin to his bedroom. Rita followed him quietly. She sensed his wolf was on edge.

"Take your clothes off." He ordered as he unbuttoned his jeans and zipped them down. Rita looked at him with wide eyes. Seeing her hesitation, he came to stand in front of her.

"You can take it off, or I can." He rumbled. Staring into his eyes, Rita removed the leather halter dress she was wearing, letting it slide off her body and to the ground. Jayce looked her up and down, his stare heating her up from the inside out.

"You're the most beautiful wolf I've ever laid eyes on." He told her.

"And it pisses me off that no one can smell me on you, that no one knows you're mine. I intend to change that." His eyes flashed wolf before he had her pinned against the wall.

"Just say no if you don't want this." He breathed as he raked his canines along her neck. Say no? Was he crazy? How could she say no when this was the attention she'd been craving from him?

"It's all I've ever wanted once I knew you were mine," she said. Jayce left her neck and gazed into her eyes. Rita knew they were glowing, letting him know just how much she desired him. He placed his finger under her chin and picked her head up slightly. He slowly leaned forward as if taunting her before he finally laid his lips on hers. Rita gasped and moaned slightly as he pecked at her lips. The moment she opened her mouth to moan, he slipped her his tongue and clasped his hand around the back of her neck. He kissed her deeply, sucking her tongue and nipping at her succulent lips. Unable to contain himself, Jayce pulled from her lips and immediately dropped to his knees in front of her. He picked her legs up and held them against the wall. Her flexibility allowed him to be able to hold her wide open.

Her lush insides winked at him. She was shining with arousal. Jayce leaned forward and ran his tongue over her folds. Her body twitched against the wall, but Jayce held tight to her. He made a grunt of pleasure before he began sucking at her lips, drawing them into his mouth slow and rhythmically. She tasted so good, Jayce had to question whether he needed any other meal for the rest of his life. Feeling her tremble in his hands amped him up to suck harder, lick faster, and twirl his tongue over her growing bud to see her come to release, and when she came, it was magical.

Her juices squirted back into Jayce's mouth, and he happily slurped them up. He stuck his tongue down her channel and fucked her until she shook uncontrollably. She was tapping on the wall furiously. When he didn't listen to her tap out, she dug her claws into his back. He finally retreated, pulling from her gushing pussy. Still holding her legs up, he placed them in the crook of his arms and carried her to his bed. He dumped her down softly. On the fall, she closed her legs, but Jayce leaned forward and pushed them back open.

"Don't move." He ordered with a brow raised. She tilted her head up and gave him a low growl but listened to what he said. Slowly, with her eyes on him, he pulled his jeans down. Her chest began to rise and fall faster when he began stripping from his underwear. Rita became apprehensive when she saw the length hanging from his hips. She'd been around shifters to know that most of them were blessed in ways humans couldn't even fathom, but just because she was a shifter herself, didn't mean she could always handle what male shifters had to offer. She wasn't a virgin, but she wasn't exactly experienced.

"Jayce, I-" He spanked her on the thigh.

"What did I say about moving?" he asked. Rita opened her legs again, pressing them against her chest. It was hard to just lay there wide open knowing he was glaring directly at her. It was a sense of vulnerability that Rita didn't know how to handle, but she also knew that he was testing her ability to submit to him. If she couldn't allow her guards to be down, then they had no right to be mated, so no matter how embarrassed she was, she just laid there wide open for him.

"What's the matter?" he asked her.

"I don't know if I can handle it," she replied quietly. Jayce pulled her down towards the edge of the bed and curled her more into a ball. He leaned against the back of her thighs with the fat head of his erection resting at her opening.

"We were destined for each other, weren't we?" he questioned.

"Yes." The words tumbled out of her mouth shakily as he pressed his head into her opening. Already, she could feel the incredible stretch that he was going to subject her to.

"So, that means your body was made to handle mine, sweetie." He pushed further. Rita moaned out in both pleasure and pain, and he continued to delve deep inside her slowly.

"Relax your hips," he said softly stopping only for a minute. Rita closed her eyes and took a deep breath. On the exhale, she opened her eyes and relaxed her hips. The moment she did, he continued to press inside her.

"You okay?" he asked as he began stroking her. Rita answered him by letting out a deep moan. She shut her eyes as pleasure assaulted her body. She should have told him she never had a g-spot orgasm just so, he understood why she was about to lose control as if she was having an exorcism.

"Jesus, Rita." He groaned. Her insides fisted him and coated him heavily in juices that allowed him to glide within her, even though she was tighter than a vice. By her body's response, he could sense that she hadn't felt this kind of pleasure before. It gave his wolf much needed comfort knowing that he was the one who could please their mate. As her body twitched over and over with orgasms, Jayce continued to push her further into a ball, increasing the pace of his thrusts.

"Don't stop," she begged. She was having orgasms like she was driving over a parking lot lined with speed bumps. It was continuous, and Jayce's thrusts were evenly paced and hard enough to blow her open. Their eyes connected and zinged as they glowed together. Jayce unsheathed his claws and dragged them along her side and over her hips deeply marking her. She repeated the gesture, clawing him under his V-line and over his hips. Instead of completing the mating with a bite, the claw marks would ensure that other wolves were aware that they were indeed marked by their mates.

Feeling her claws dig into his skin broke his threshold. He shouted out and pounded into her body relentlessly, holding her tight in a ball so she couldn't squirm away from him. Even though she was apprehensive at first, now her pussy was gushing and trembling with excitement.

"All mine." He gritted as he erupted inside of her. She screamed out his name as she accepted the product of his gender deep within her.

"Shit." Rita breathed. Her body was zinging and pulsing with gratification. Jayce slowly let her legs down, but he never moved from atop her. He hovered over, keeping their bodies connected. Truthfully, Jayce couldn't pull from her body yet. She just felt too good.

"I may need a moment to heal before we go for round two," she said softly, smiling at him. Jayce kissed her on the mouth before flipping them over. He landed on his back and kept her seated on his length on top of him. He placed his hands behind his back.

"Whenever you're ready, baby. My dick ain't goin' nowhere." Rita giggled. Even though she said she needed a moment, being on top of him sparked something in her lower belly, and she couldn't help but start to grind her hips back and forth.

"There you go, my wolf," he coaxed, rubbing her hips.

"It's yours all night if you want it." Rita took that sentiment to heart because she realized she was never going to be nowhere near done with him.

****

Rita awoke with her body swirling with pleasure. She smiled and stretched ready to reach for Jayce. Her smile slipped from her face when she realized he wasn't next to her. After a long night of lovemaking, she expected to wake up next to her mate, but he was long gone. By sniffing the air, she smelled the residual scent of him, but nothing was new. Getting up from the soft bed, Rita stretched and went to take care of her hygiene. After brushing her teeth and getting a shower, she decided to utilize the open space behind Jayce's cabin and let her wolf out to stretch. In her wolf form outside, she tilted her nose up to the sky and was able to smell her mate nearby. Eager to see him, Rita hurriedly shifted back and dressed in a loose sundress the alpha female had lent to her seeing that Rita wasn't traveling with much clothes, to begin with. When she was dressed, she rushed out of the cabin to find her mate.

Rita smelled her mate clear as day, but the further she walked to it, the more his scent got tangled up with other scents. Female scents. Her wolf was on alert already, baring its teeth, and she was right to do so. Rita halted when she spotted Jayce standing next to three she-wolves. She fought her own wolf, so the animal didn't come leaping out ready to show her possessiveness over her mate. They hadn't mated officially last night, so their scents were not mixed, but with the amount of sex they had last night, the she-wolves should be able to smell her on him. Just like any male could smell Jayce had been all over her.

"Be calm, be calm," Rita murmured to herself as she walked up to them. Sneaking up wasn't something she could do. Jayce sensed his mate immediately and looked towards her. She was glaring at him as she walked up to him. He knew she was holding tightly to her wolf to not let the beast out.

"Hey," she said tightly.

"Hey, Rita. You know Shelly, Dion, and Kyra?" Jayce pointed out the three wolves. Of the three, Kyra was the only one that smiled at her and waved. Rita reciprocated the gesture but scowled at the other two.

"Shelly is the one I told you about who when I tried talking to her, she kind of blew me off. I actually didn't even get a chance to figure out her name until just now."

"Really?" Jayce looked at Shelly.

"I've talked to you about your attitude." Jayce scolded her.

"What am I supposed to do? She was an omega for a reason."

"You can start off by not being a bitch," Kyra said. Shelly rolled her eyes. When she looked at Rita, she took a long sniff.

"Can you excuse us? We were talking about something that doesn't include you." Rita crossed her arms and planted her feet not intending to leave.

"You know, just because you were fucking the Beta of the pack, doesn't make you any more important than the rest of the she-wolves who want to fuck him," Shelly said, so she indeed smelled Jayce on her.

"Are you challenging me?" Rita asked her lowly.

"Sounds like you are."

"Winner gets to spend a night alone with Jayce?" Shelly asked popping out her claws. Rita's eyes glowed, and she growled and lunged for Shelly. Jayce intervened, blocking Rita immediately. Shelly scurried off.

"Better watch your back!" she shouted at Rita.

"Let me get her!" Rita growled at Jayce trying to fight him off her.

"Let it go, Rita." He ordered. Rita pushed at him before slapping him across the face. He let her go but shoved her back and stood in her way not giving her a clear pass to run after Shelly.

"What the fuck was that?" She snapped at him.

"What was what?"

"I'm your mate! You just let her talk any kind of way to me?"

"She'll be dealt with. There are pack rules against starting fights and confrontations, Rita."

"I don't care about that! If someone disrespects me, Jayce, I expect my mate to have my back!"

"I will always have your back, Rita, but as the Beta, I need to maintain a certain level of neutrality. If I would have snapped at her for the way she talked to you, she could report that to Kameron, and then my position here would be at risk." Rita just stared at him.

"But last night when that wolf tried to touch me, you weren't neutral, now were you?"

"That was different. He was going to touch you, and he's male. He'll still get punished for it though. There's pack rules against what he did. Shelly can say whatever she wants. She can get the punishment that will come to her. It's the touching that would be different. Had she touched you, I would have slapped her hands off you." Rita shook her head and waved him off.

"What in the hell were you talking to her about, to begin with? I can tell she's been dying to fuck you." Jayce was about to blurt something out, but to save his own life, he quickly shut his mouth. Too bad his mate was too observant for that.

"Say it," she coaxed.

"Me and Shelly have a sexual history, Rita, but I'm not the least bit interested in her. Even when we fucked, I wasn't interested. I just did it because I was lonely, and she was available." Rita crossed her arms. "Anytime I talk to her, it's regarding pack business, and I wouldn't disrespect you by casually talking to a wolf I know doesn't want to keep things platonic with me. I suppose she just wants the position."

"What position? Your girlfriend or something?"

"No. Beta." Rita tilted her head to the side, not understanding.

"What kind of pack did you come from, Rita?" he asked.

"An unorganized, hot mess, unruly, reckless ass pack," she replied.

"In standard packs, most positions come in twos. You know, like the Alpha pair? Kameron is the Alpha, and his mate naturally would be the female alpha. In our case, I'm the Beta, so when we mate, you will also be the Beta."

"Wait, me? The Beta? I don't want to be the beta. I'm not into the politics. You know, like going around and talking to pack members and shadowing the alpha."

"Well, you better get into it, Rita, because when you carry my bite, the job is yours. That's the way it works."

"No, I don't think so, and what are you going to do when we have pups? Leave early in the morning and do pack business until all hours of the night and not spend time with me or the babies?" Jayce's eyes bulged from his head.

"PUPS?!" he exclaimed. "Whoa, cool it."

"What for? Kellan is the son of the Alpha's, which means everyone else can have pups now. Why can't we?"

"Because we only found each other a month ago. I want pups, Rita, just not now. I want to enjoy being with my mate before we have any pups, and I can't give up my position as the Beta right now either."

"But I thought…we'd start a family," she whispered. Before he could answer, she continued.

"When I go into heat, what are you going to do?" she asked.

"Just watch me in pain because you don't want to make pups with me?"

"I'd never just watch you in pain," he said.

"So, what would you do when I go into heat, huh?" She snapped.

"Going into heat doesn't guarantee pups, Rita," he said. "And I can satisfy your heating without making pups with you. Do you want to be a nursing mother while you're learning the roles of the Beta in the first place?"

"I told you I didn't want to be a Beta, Jayce!"

"You don't have a choice, Rita. Unless you're not trying to mate with me. Marking each other and solidifying the mating bond will transfer my role and power to you. I took a vow and shared blood with the Alpha and pack members. You'll be bound to the duties of a Beta the moment we mate. That's just the way it is, so saying you don't want to be a Beta is you saying you don't want to be my mate."

"You can relinquish your role, you know? You can give up the position. I thought that's what you'd do."

"I thought you'd want to be the Beta alongside with me." He countered. Rita shook her head and began to back up.

"Guess we were both wrong." She breathed. After gazing at him for a moment, she turned away and walked off. Jayce didn't stop her because he needed time to think about everything, but in hindsight, he should have stopped her. None of them thought that tragedy would strike only a few days later, leaving him and his mate unsure of their future.

Chapter One

Jayce rose from his bed like a vampire awakening for the night. It was dark in his room in the cave that his new pack now occupied. The memory of how he'd met his mate and where they left off before things went to hell haunted him. The sound of her howling out to him for him to save her from her captors scarred him and fueled his anger. Sliding out of bed, Jayce went to empty his body of fluids. In the large bathroom, he looked in the mirror. Bags hung under his eyes. He couldn't even remember when he'd gotten any kind of sleep. How long had it been since his mate was gone? To Jayce, it seemed like an eternity, but truthfully, only a week had gone by, but it was the worst week of his life. He touched the claw marks Rita had marked him with. He was thankful they would never disappear even though she was gone.

Not knowing what else to do, Jayce got dressed in cargo's and a t-shirt and strapped on his boots. Being a shifter meant that he didn't need weapons. Even if he wanted weapons, where the hell would he carry them? His teeth and claws were weapon enough, and even if he didn't know where to look, he couldn't just sit around. He had to do something that would give him insight to where the hell his mate was. He was quiet as he left his room and headed towards the exit of the cave, and though he made no sound, the moment he reached the entrance, he smelled the uniquely mixed scent of his Alpha female.

"Going somewhere this late?" she asked, stepping into the foyer of the cave. Jayce stopped walking but kept his back to her.

"You know where," Jayce replied.

"Actually, I don't," Bliss said. "Unless you figured out something, and I don't think the Beta would do something sneaky as hide or withhold information from the Alphas."

"I can't just sit around, Bliss, waiting for something to happen. I need to find her."

"We know you do, Jayce, but just going out there halfcocked not knowing where you're looking can be dangerous, and I don't know about you, but I don't want to lose you either." Jayce crossed his arms and still kept his back turned towards her.

"You may feel that way, but I gotta do what I gotta do, and that's just the way it is. You won't stop me from doing what I have to do."

"Well, since you put it that way, Jayce, I can stop you. I don't want to pull the rank card, but I'm not allowing you to go out there like that. You're not going out there tonight." Bliss pulsed her Alpha vibes at him, and his wolf bowed down to her. In any other case, his wolf would have recognized her dominant nature, but he wouldn't feel the need to obey any order she gave. Since she mated Kellan, his powers transferred to her through their bond, which meant the blood vows he took with the rest of the pack was shared with Bliss. If Kellan gave him an order, he would be inclined to obey it, and now the same went for Bliss. It was a good thing he liked her, or else he would be pissed he had to listen to her. Now he was just upset.

"Fucking hell." He grunted. Instead of turning to look at her, he went straight to one of the openings of the tunnels to go around back to his room, but before he could get far, Bliss called out to him.

"Take your anger out on me," she said. "Let's go do some training. No doubt I need a challenge like you."

Finally, Jayce turned and looked at her. She gave him a small smile, and Jayce took comfort in it. He realized she wasn't just being a bitch and using her powers because she had them. She did care, and knowing how upset he was to even train with him could be dangerous, but she was willing to do it because she knew he needed a way to let his frustration out.

"Make sure you tell Kellan this was all your idea." Jayce snorted. He turned back around and continued down the tunnel. Bliss followed him until they went around the tunnel. It took a couple of days to see how extensive the place was, and in that time, they'd found extra rooms and a set of stone stairs that led further down into the cave, but unlike the rest of the place, the lower floor wasn't furnished at all. It was simply a large space with bare rock walls. They'd been using the space for miscellaneous reasons, but since Rita was missing, Jayce had set up a punching bag that hung from the ceiling, and every night he was beating the crap out of that thing.

Bliss thought she was ready for the training session, but when Jayce turned to look at her, his wolf eyes were lighting up the cavern. Kellan's eyes were a stark blue, but Jayce's wolf eyes were an intense shade of amber. She realized then that he wasn't here to take it easy on her. All she could do was prepare herself for a good fight. She unsheathed her claws then let her canines drop from her gums. Before she could even gain a proper stance, Jayce was lunging at her. She sidestepped him like Jaxson taught her to do plenty of times and used his weight against him. Bliss was always successful when she did the same thing with Gemma or Kyra, but doing it with Jayce, he quickly reversed the move, and next thing she knew, she was on her ass with a loud thud. Thankful for her fast healing, she was up in a matter of seconds. She swung widely, but he ducked and dodged. She wasn't so lucky on dodging his hits. He caught her in the stomach with his fists and on the arms with his claws. Bliss gritted her teeth and began to fight harder swinging her claws viciously. She caught him across the face, and when he faltered, she kept attacking him.

He doubled over when she dug her claws into his chest. She noticed then that his breathing was hoarse. She backed up and watched as he took his time to straighten up. When he did, she saw that his face had changed. His brows were thick and stitched together, his nose was changed, and he had whiskers. He looked more like a werewolf than a shifter, like his wolf, was trying to break loose and the human part of Jayce wasn't letting the wolf take over, but if Jayce was still in there, Bliss couldn't see him. He glared at her, growling as he breathed heavily.

"Jayce…" Bliss breathed nervously, but he didn't answer her. He let out a deafening roar before he was charging at her. Bliss screamed and cowered ready for his attack. The intense pain she thought she was going to feel never came. Kellan burst into the cavern roaring himself. He lunged at Jayce, diverting him away from Bliss and crashing him to the stone wall. Jayce fell to the ground where Kellan hovered over him and let out a thunderous roar. Even though she was part of the Alpha, his roar was enough to wake up her wolf. She fought against shifting to howl with her Alpha. Jayce howled back before his body was contorting and changing. The features of his werewolf blended back into his face, and his wolf eyes tinkered out slowly, returning back to his human eyes. He jumped up quickly like he was snapped from a trance. He looked between Kellan and Bliss, shock on his face.

"Kellan, I-I blacked out; I didn't intentionally attack her." He spoke up. Bliss saw her mate's chest rising and falling, and with their bond, she sensed his deep anger. Kellan turned to look at her.

"Are you out of your mind?" he asked.

"Me?" Bliss exclaimed. "He's the one that went crazy, and we were just training!"

"He's going through the loss of his mate right now. This is not a wolf you want to be training with. He's too on edge, and anything can set him off."

"How did you even know this was happening?" Bliss asked. "When I left bed, you were fast asleep."

"I sensed your fear through the bond, and then I felt something was wrong with Jayce." He looked over at Jayce who was sitting stoically with his back against the cave wall.

"Let's go, Bliss. Jayce needs time alone."

"No, he doesn't." Bliss countered. "He's had enough of that. Let me talk to him alone."

"He just tried to harm you, Bliss."

"I'm not worried." Kellan knew Jayce would never purposely hurt his mate, but Jayce's control wasn't at its normal. Kellan supposed he'd feel the same way if something had happened to Bliss, and he had no way of fixing it. Jayce looked up at Kellan, and their eyes connected. He saw the remorse Jayce felt for losing control and attacking his mate, and Kellan couldn't hold a grudge against him.

"I'll be around," Kellan said backing away. Before he left, he kissed Bliss on the cheek to appease his wolf. When he left the cavern, Bliss walked up to Jayce slowly. She sat in front of him so he knew she didn't fear he would lunge at her again.

"I knew this was a bad idea." He grunted. "I nearly killed you."

"I don't think you would have gotten that far," Bliss said. "Besides, that's why we heal."

"We heal from many things, Bliss, but having your heart shredded by claws isn't one of those things." Bliss shrugged.

"I'll never forgive myself for what happened with Rita." Bliss spoke softly.

"It's not your fault, and you shouldn't carry that blame on yourself. If only I'd mated her." Jayce shook his head.

"What do you mean?"

"If I mated her, then we'd be fully bonded. Then I would be able to find her or at least know what she's going through. If she's dead, I wouldn't even be able to tell. I can't feel anything for my mate simply because I didn't complete our bond."

"Why didn't you mate? Here I was thinking that a mating would naturally happen anytime a wolf met his mate."

"It should naturally happen with wolves, but sometimes, there's special circumstances. I didn't know Rita when I found out she was my mate so here's this strange woman that comes along, and my wolf claims her. Being connected to my wolf for as long as I've been alive, me and my wolf almost always want the same thing, so when I saw Rita, it was like someone punched me in my gut, and both me and my wolf wanted her immediately."

"I don't think anything can be worse than how I acted with Kellan. I was sniffing his beard and kissing on him like I knew him for years."

"It happens like that, and since the moment I met her, we spent a month and a half just getting to know each other. The both of us want to mate, Bliss. There's no doubt about it. We just have-" Jayce shook his head.

"What?" Bliss asked.

"I don't wanna talk about it anymore," he said.

"Just know that I regret not mating her when I had the chance." Bliss rubbed his back.

"I feel terrible for giving Rita hell." Bliss spoke up. Jayce looked at her.

"I kept accusing her of wanting Kellan and sleeping with him, and I had no clue she wouldn't even bat an eye at him because she had you." Jayce grunted and got up from the ground. His eyes had gone back wolf, and Bliss feared she said the wrong thing.

"Jayce…" Bliss got up to follow him.

"Leave me alone, Bliss." He growled. He stormed out of the cavern and kept walking until he disappeared around the tunnel in the direction of his room. Hearing what Bliss said, Jayce was reminded of how Rita had chosen to leave the pack and go find Kellan to be with him instead of staying with Jayce. Logically, it was safer for Rita to be away from Maverick, but Jayce didn't want his mate away from him, especially to be with another wolf, so instead of being around Bliss to possibly take his anger out on her again, he went back to his room where he punched the stone walls until his knuckles opened up and bled profusely.

Chapter Two

Rita screamed as someone burned the wolfsbane out of her body. Purple smoke permeated the cell she was locked away in as the poison was forced from her body, and when it was all over, Rita laid limply on the stone floor with sweat pebbling her face and body.

"How does that feel?" a soft voice asked. Rita could barely open her eyes. Pain was slithering throughout her whole body, but she remembered everything. She remembered being captured after the attack on her pack. She remembered watching Jayce go down with wolfs bane shot into him. Immediately, Rita gritted her teeth and tried to shift. Pain racked her body causing her to scream out. Inside her, her wolf whined and pawed at the magical barriers between their souls. The wolf couldn't get out. Rita tried shifting again but was only met with more gut-wrenching pain. Tears streamed down her face. Why was this happening?

"Please, don't cry." The voice sounded again. Rita sniffled. Her eyes creaked open, but everything was dark. She inhaled. She wasn't alone. In fact, there was more than just one wolf, and they were all females. Rita forced her eyes to adjust to the darkness. Once she did, she understood why she couldn't shift. Her feet and her hands were adorned by silver metal cuffs. Just like a silver bullet could kill a wolf, anything silver prevented a wolf from healing and having the ability to shift, and the longer a wolf had silver on, the more their powers were drained. Rita sat up slowly, and gritted her teeth to the pain lancing through her body. There were three other females in the cell with her and all three of them had silver cuffs around their wrists and ankles. The female closest to Rita was the one burning out the wolfs bane from Rita's body. She was young. All three of them were.

"Do you still feel the poison?" she asked. Rita shook her head.

"It's not there, but my body can't heal completely because of the cuffs."

"That's how we all feel." One of the other wolves spoke up.

"Do any of you know where we are?" Rita asked. All of them shook their heads.

"We've been here for a week almost, but we know nothing else."

"What's your names?" Rita asked.

"Brandy." The wolf closest to Rita spoke. The other two on the far side got a little bit closer to Rita.

"That's Amber, and she's Maya."

"My name is Rita." The four of them smiled to each other in a sense of comradery.

"Do you remember how you got here?" Rita asked. Maya spoke.

"We're all from the same pack. Everything was going like normal, and the next thing I know, the elders were screaming, and we heard fighting. We were told to run and not come back."

"Before we got far, we were shot with wolfsbane." Amber continued. "Then it was lights out, and we woke up in here."

"Oh, my God." Rita gasped.

"We don't know what happened to our pack or why we're even here." Brandy shrugged.

"But some fucktard named Maverick says we're part of his pack now." Rita clenched her fists.

"Maverick attacked my pack too, but his men only took me. I think they were planning to take more of my sister wolves, they didn't have the chance."

"We're scared." Maya admitted.

"Our pack is mostly elders, and we hardly have any trouble. The Alpha was really hurt when we ran off. We're scared he might be dead." Rita could confirm what she sensed. They were young.

"Well, when pack members die, especially the Alpha, you should be able to feel it. Come over here." The three girls gathered around her.

"Close your eyes and imagine your Alpha. Remember how it felt when you pledged your vow to him. Single out his essence, his spirit inside you." The three wolves were quiet as they did what Rita said. Rita did the same thing herself. She felt Kellan's strong pulse, coupled with Bliss'. They'd mated. Happiness floored through her, excited for the Alpha pair. It meant their pack would only get stronger with two fierce Alphas to lead them.

"I feel him." Maya spoke up excitedly.

"It's like a pulse, but it's weak, but does that mean he's alive?"

"Yes, that's exactly what it means," Rita said. "As long as you feel that pulse, you know your Alpha is still alive, and it means he's doing whatever he can to make sure the three of you are rescued."

"What about you?" Amber asked quietly.

"I'm sure my pack will stop at nothing to find me," Rita said softly.

"But while we wait to be rescued, we can't be complacent. We too have to fight back."

"Fight?" Maya's voice was shaky.

"Yes, fight, but don't worry, I've got your back, trust me." The three wolves nodded at Rita gaining confidence in their alliance.

"Someone's coming." Brandy alerted them. They sat next to each other facing the opening of the cell. Rita scented Maverick immediately, but she could feel her enhanced abilities begin to dim. She didn't know what lay in store for them, but if it included Maverick, it was not going to be pretty.

"Get up." Maverick demanded when he opened the metal bars. Rita led the wolves to standing up. Even if they were afraid, Rita didn't want to give Maverick that satisfaction. When they stood, Maverick looked all four of them up and down, evaluating them. He scented each one of them.

"Who had their heat cycle already?" Maverick asked.

"We all did." Brandy spoke up. "We had our second full moon shifting just days ago when you decided to attack our pack." Maverick waved her off and looked at Rita.

"You haven't gone into heat." He accused, pointing a finger at her.

"And?" Rita asked.

"You're gonna keep me locked away here waiting for my cycle?"

"Oh, I'm sure we'll have some fun in the time being." Rita glared at him trying to show she wasn't afraid.

"Now, I don't like treating my own kind like garbage, so if we can come to an agreement, I will gladly move you all to a nice bedroom upstairs." The young wolves were surprised, and a spark of happiness hit them, but Rita wasn't fooled.

"Wait a minute, what's the catch here, huh?" she asked.

"What's the point of you keeping us here? Whether in a nice room or a cell, you're still keeping us a prisoner, so what the fuck are you planning?"

"In due time, sweetheart." Maverick smiled.

"And this is your new home, Rita. I am your Alpha, so you'd better start showing me some respect." Rita scoffed.

"We both know who's my Alpha, and the moment he finds me, he's gonna rip you to shreds. Not only that, but Kellan's a mated Alpha, which means he's more powerful, and if you couldn't beat him when he wasn't mated, imagine now that he is mated. You're living on borrowed time, asshole." Maverick's canine dropped in his anger.

"See, I'm trying to be the reputable wolf, but you she-wolves keep testing me. I'll have to remind you, Rita, that I'm not the Alpha you wanna fuck with." He looked at the three young wolves.

"Someone will come and bring you three to the bedroom. I want you showered, hair done, and dressed in the outfits that will be brought to you. As for you, Rita, let's get reacquainted." Maverick grabbed her by the back of her neck, digging his claws into her flesh. With his strength, he led her out of the cell. Rita was surprised that the cell was located in the basement of house. She thought for sure they were in some kind of cave. Maverick led her up a spiral stone staircase. The first floor of the house was luxurious, and as he took her to the next floor, she could see this wasn't just a regular house. It was a mansion. Wolves had their own means of money, but Rita never met a wolf who wanted to live in a mansion or even had enough money to keep up with it. This meant that Maverick was into some serious business to keep such a steady income.

Maverick pushed her into a large bedroom. Laying on the large bed was Hera like she was some form of royalty or something.

"Kellan isn't the only one with a woman at his side." Maverick told her.

"Kellan doesn't just have a woman at his side. He has his mate," Rita said. "That is in no comparison to your fuck buddy over here."

"I hope you're putting her to work tonight," Hera stated. Rita gave her a look.

"Putting me to work?" she asked.

"I'm in sort of a dilemma here." Maverick spoke. He went over to his mini bar and poured himself some whiskey. Rita understood that shifters drank for leisure and for the taste of the liquor because there was nothing that could get a shifter drunk.

"I'm trying to have the most powerful pack not only in the city, or the state. I'm talking 'bout the whole world. What do you think I'm missing?"

"A pair of balls," Rita answered. Maverick turned around and backhanded her. She stumbled a little, but the sting of the slap dissipated almost immediately. Blood coated her mouth but she didn't show any form of weakness. Though the silver cuffs were keeping her wolf locked inside her, she would still be able to heal minor pains. Though Rita began to suspect that the longer she was in the cuffs the weaker she would eventually become.

"I'm gonna warn you, Rita. Keep talking to me like that, and you won't like what happens to you." He scowled.

"So, I guess that's what you did to Bliss, huh? She spoke her mind, and you slapped her around knowing damn well she was human and in no way capable of defending herself against you? I may have these cuffs on, Maverick, but I'm not human. Your little bitch slaps ain't gonna make me cower."

"Funny you should bring that up." He went quiet, and Rita got the feeling that he was mind speaking with someone, and a moment later, two males came into the bedroom.

"The thing is, Rita, in order to be the strongest pack, I, of course, need to reproduce strong pups of my own blood, but I realize that I can't be the supreme Alpha if I have other Alphas trying to take what is mine. Your Alpha happens to be one of those wolves who won't let me be. Now that I have you here, you're going to tell me how to find where it is your Alpha is hiding. Strap her up." Before Rita could defend herself, the two males that had entered the room lunged at her. One of them captured her hands while the other injected her with a needle. Rita went weak immediately. By the purple vapors that came out of the injection site, she knew it was wolfs bane, and with the silver cuffs on, the wolfs bane easily weakened her further. Rita felt like she was sinking into a deep abyss, and then everything went dark.

Chapter Three

Kellan paced back and forth in the room they had designated to hold their meetings. Bliss, Jaxson, and Tristan sat around the round table watching Kellan. They were waiting for Jayce to arrive in the room. Kellan checked his watch for the fifth time. He was about to growl for his Beta to get his ass to the room, but the doors burst open, and Jayce came in. His knuckles were bleeding again but slowly healing. His eyes were flashing wolf, but the moment he came into the room and sensed Bliss, his human eyes came back. After he nearly attacked her, Kellan figured he was stifling his wolf as much as he could to not have the same thing happening again.

"Sorry I'm late." He gritted out. "I um-lost control again." He took his place around the table next to Kellan's seat. Bliss sat on the other side of Kellan.

"Jayce, if you have to take time off from your duties, then I'll understand that," Kellan said. "But attacking my mate, being late to meetings, and continuously not having control of your wolf are things I cannot tolerate, Jayce, so if you-"

"I can handle it," Jayce said. "I admit to my control issues, and for attacking your mate, I will face those consequences, but I took a vow, and I don't plan on letting this unqualify me for my position."

"Pack vote," Kellan said. "Is Jayce in or out?" Kellan went around the table taking votes to see if the pack believed he could still perform even though Rita was missing. No one voted against him.

"Alright, you're in," Kellan said.

"But you're not allowed to be with any of the she-wolves alone. Especially Gemma and my mate."

"Why especially Gemma?" Tristan grunted.

"She recently shifted for the first time. She has no control over her wolf as of yet. Same thing for Bliss. The way I see it, Jayce can't control his wolf, and neither can Gemma. Her wolf is naturally on edge, and if any wolf comes at her in a wrong way, it won't be good. If they start snapping at each other, we're gonna have a full-blown fight on our hands." Everyone nodded in agreement understanding what Kellan meant.

"Fine," Jayce said. "I can agree to those terms. What about the consequence of what I did to Bliss?"

"We'll talk privately about that," Kellan replied. Even though Kellan wasn't trying to be a strict Alpha, all packs had rules, and breaking them meant consequences. That was just the way of the pack.

"Updates on security." Kellan nodded towards Tristan. He cleared his throat and looked through the small notebook he had in front of him.

"I installed new security systems through the cave. The front main door opens to the touch of the pack only, so a finger, a palm, whatever it is, it'll open to the pack members. I already set my palm print, and it works fine, so I'll need the rest of the members to set up their prints as well. I purchased some cameras for the surrounding areas so we can keep watch. I'll have to set them up in one of the spare rooms soon."

"Okay, I want that done asap. After the meeting, Bliss, get Kyra and Gemma and get their prints scanned in." Bliss nodded. "How much did you pay for the cameras?"

"The cameras plus the monitors all for about 2 grand. I got a friend that owns an electronic shop. He gave me a good deal." Kellan nodded.

"I set up a pack bank account," Kellan said. "Jayce, you and I have control over the account. I put both our names on the paperwork. We have about 20 grand in there of pack money; most of which my parents left me. I'll wire you back your money Tristan for the equipment."

"You don't have to," Tristan said. "I'm part of the pack and we all pay our dues in some way. And I'll use my own money for the protection of my pack."

"Thanks," Kellan nodded. "Anything else?"

"The she-wolves. We should be monitoring when they come and go," Tristan said. "Especially with someone like Maverick out there kidnapping women."

"What? You want us to start asking permission to come and go?" Bliss asked.

"You know that's not what I mean, but in times like this, I'd like to know where my female pack members are if I'm supposed to be protecting them," Tristan said.

"None of us have even been going anywhere. The only place we've been is the natural springs on the other side of the cave which still protects us because, with the waterfall, our scent can't be detected."

"You get my point though right, Kellan?" Tristan asked.

"Yes, I do , but the she-wolves also have a right to their privacy, so we'll have to discuss some ways to keep them safe out there and to make sure they aren't followed when they return back here." Tristan and Bliss nodded ending that topic.

"Any reports?" Kellan asked looking at Jayce waiting for his Beta report.

"The pack that Gemma's parents have been taken too, I haven't been able to get back in contact with them. I tried calling both Gabe and Gina and got nothing. I've phoned their Alpha and got no answer. I'm wondering if we should go back to their land and figure out what's been going on."

"How long has it been?" Kellan asked.

"For as long as Rita's been gone, which is a couple of days, almost a week now. The question is, should we go on a search or not?"

"Me and you can go on a search," Kellan said after thinking. "That way Tristan and Jaxson can stay here and man the fort."

"I understand we need to protect other packs, Kellan, but right now, we're missing our own pack member." Jaxson spoke up.

"Our energy needs to be wholly on finding Rita, and afterwards, we can help other packs. I don't see how we can provide any help when we ourselves are scrambling because of what Maverick did."

"He's right," Bliss murmured.

"I know, but Gemma's parents are part of that pack."

"And if anything were wrong with them, Gemma would be able to sense it." Jaxson added. Kellan nodded.

"Alright. When we find Rita, we will deal with everything else."

"The question is, how do we find her?" Tristan asked.

"We've been all over these woods, and we can't get one single trace of her scent."

Jayce took a deep breath. His claws were elongating, so he put his hands under the table and dug them into the flesh of his thighs. Inflicting pain on himself somehow was the answer to keeping him calm.

"She's not dead, is she?" Jayce asked Kellan.

"No," Kellan replied. "I can still feel her. She's very much alive." As the Alpha, Kellan felt every one of his pack mates, and he knew when things went bad with them. For Rita, he felt her pulse, and that's it. Nothing else.

"Have you tried projecting to her?" Kellan asked.

"I've tried. She hasn't responded, and I didn't receive any messages. It's like I can't sense her period. Both me and my wolf don't know what to do."

"Wait. If you two didn't complete the bond, then how come you're not in pain?" Bliss questioned.

"Because we marked each other," Jayce said.

"My wolf can be content about that, and I don't feel physical pain."

"Thank goodness for-" Bliss hissed and clenched her fists. Pain lanced through her body, but it didn't come from a clear direction. Kellan looked at her immediately.

"Baby?" he asked. Bliss stood slowly as the sharp pain zinged through her again. Her claws began to elongate, and her eyes lit up.

"Bliss, what's the matter?" Kellan asked. Kellan instantly felt the burning of the pain his mate was feeling through their bond, but oddly, though she was experiencing the pain, it wasn't hers.

"I can't control my wolf." Bliss grunted as her canine's filled her mouth. The pain of whatever was happening to her was enough for her wolf to push at her walls trying to protect her from the pain. Kellan scooped her in his arms and quickly ran out of the room heading towards the workout space beneath the living quarters, so Bliss had a safe place to shift. Her bones shifted while in his arms. By the time he reached the bottom level and dropped her to the ground, her wolf came bursting out ready to attack. Kellan growled at her, and she heeled immediately, but the wolf was not ready to let Bliss out, so she just paced the room, but it seemed the moment Bliss shifted, the pain she was feeling switched onto Kellan. Because of the connection with his wolf, he knew how to maintain the beast on the onslaught of the pain and not feel the need to shift. Anyone as new as Bliss wouldn't be able to control their animal. Kellan winced at the pain piercing throughout his body.

"What the hell is going on?" Jaxson asked seeing both his alphas being affected by something. Kellan looked at Jayce.

"It's Rita," Kellan said.

"She's in pain and a lot of it. Me and Bliss both felt it."

Jayce lasted a total of three seconds before he completely lost it. He roared as his beast tore from his body. Kellan shifted just as quickly to protect his mate from the feral wolf.

****

Rita clenched her teeth as pain seared throughout her body. Sweat rolled down her heated skin as she bore through the pain being inflicted. Her wolf was constantly pouncing forward trying to emerge to protect Rita, but the silver cuffs kept the wolf chained inside.

"Where's the pack now?" Maverick asked her evenly. Rita took raspy breaths with her head hung down. Her arms were suspended above her head shackled together with her feet dangling off the ground. After she'd awoken from the poison in her bloodstream, she was in another bedroom, and the questioning began.

"Fuck off." Rita spat out. She clenched her teeth as the leather strap Maverick wielded smacked against her skin. She didn't know what the strap looked like, but she was aware that her skin was being torn open, and it wasn't healing like it should. She had no clue where the new pack land was, but she would rather show her allegiance to her pack by telling Maverick to fuck off rather than she just didn't know.

"It's been three hours, Rita. Still wanna be defiant?" Maverick asked.

"Might as well just kill me." She shrugged. "Because I'm not telling you where my pack is." Maverick twirled his fingers through her locks before inhaling them.

"You can try to keep them from me, but I will find them and kill them all." Since she was naked dangling in front of him, Maverick stood and looked over her body. He kneeled down and sniffed the claw marks across her hip. It was the mark of a mate. Inhaling, he smiled and looked at her.

"Jayce, huh?" he questioned. "Didn't know the two of you were a thing." Rita didn't answer him.

"Does he know I wanted you to have my pups, and that's why you ran off to find Kellan?" Again, Rita was silent. Maverick laughed sensing that there was much Jayce didn't know.

"Well, here's what I'm going to do," Maverick said.

"I'm gonna find your little pack. Take back my bitch, Bliss, take you, and Gemma, hell even Kyra, and I'll put my pups in all four of you, and then I'll kill your Alpha, Beta, and the enforcers, and then I'll go around making sure that every female wolf within fifty miles of here is having pups by me. Because then, even when I die, my bloodline will see no end."

"You're a psycho," Rita mumbled out.

"Aw, thanks." Maverick smiled. "I think you've had enough for one night. We will resume again, and if I were you, I wouldn't resist for too long. I don't plan on lightening up."

"Neither do I," Rita said. The two male wolves that had drugged her came into the room again.

"Bring her to the room with the others." Maverick ordered. The both of them stalked over to Rita. She hung there limply, but her mind was moving a mile a minute.

"She's real cute this one," he said rubbing his hand along Rita's thigh. Rita glared at him, and when he ran his hand on the inside of her thigh, Rita popped her legs up and wrapped them around his arm. She twisted and popped his arm from his socket. It was a neat little trick that Jaxson taught her, and with much practice, she could twist anything with her legs and break it. The wolf howled out in pain and fell to the ground holding his broken arm. The other wolf was ready to slap Rita across the face, but Maverick stopped him.

"No one is allowed to touch my girls," Maverick stated.

"Punishment is left up to me. Got that, Levi?"

"Yeah, I got it, but what about Rory?" Levi asked. Maverick shrugged.

"That's what he gets for touching her. Next time he'll think twice." Rory growled as he sat up and popped his arm back into place.

"Now, get her to the room like I asked." Maverick looked at Rita one last time before he left the room. Though she was at his mercy, there was no weakness in her eyes. He had said that he was not going to give in, and he realized then that Rita wasn't going to give in either. What worried Maverick was that not only was Kellan going to be at his back to rescue Rita, but if Jayce was truly her mate, Maverick was going to have to deal with more than just an Alpha. He was going to have to deal with a rogue shifter who would do anything to save his mate.

Rita grunted as Rory and Levi tossed her inside another bedroom. She refused to show weakness, so she kept her grunt as low as possible. She turned around and growled at the two wolves. They simply growled back before leaving the room.

"Rita!" Brandy gasped. Her, Maya, and Amber rushed to her side to help her up to her feet.

"What have they been doing to you?" Amber asked.

"Trying to get information on my pack. Maverick thinks torturing me will get me to talk. He has another thing coming for sure." Rita looked at the girls and realized what they had on. She gasped and touched the skimpy material.

"Is this the shit they wanted you to wear?" Rita asked. Maya nodded and looked at the teddy she was wearing.

"There's one for you too," Maya said nodding over to the bed. Rita eyed the black and white slutty maid outfit. Knowing that Maverick wanted to breed every she-wolf in his path, the outfits made sense.

"This is some bullshit." Rita gritted. She winced at the pain lancing through her body.

"Let us help you clean up." Brandy offered. "You must be in terrible pain."

"I'm fine." Rita lied. "I'll go clean up." Rita left the young wolves and limped towards the bathroom. When she closed the door and locked herself inside, she let out a quivering breath. The luxurious bathroom was decked out in white and pink towels with both a jacuzzi tub and a shower stall. There was a floor to ceiling mirror that Rita slowly walked up to. Her heart beat loudly in anticipation for what she was going to see when she looked at herself. The tears she'd been holding back in front of Maverick slowly slipped from her eyes when she saw the long lashes and welts all over her skin. Like she felt, the wounds hadn't healed the way they should of.

Each mark was seeping blood, leaving long streams traveling down her naked body. She touched Jayce's claw marks on her hips. It looked like now after the beating Maverick put her through, Jayce's marks weren't going to be the only permanent thing on her body. With her hand still on Jayce's mating mark, she sniffled and turned to the standing shower and turned on the water. She wished that Jayce and the rest of the pack were going to come bursting through the walls of wherever the hell this mansion was and coming to save her for the pure hell that Maverick had in store for her and the other wolves.

As the warm water stung her wounds, she hissed but kept herself from making any other sound. The worst thing she could do at the moment was show her weakness with three other young wolves who were scared themselves, so she sucked up her tears. An image of Jayce's smile came into her head, and she felt herself cracking a small smirk remembering how handsome he was when he smiled. She knew it was a longshot, but in her head, she called out his name.

Jayce? She waited, holding her breath, but after a moment, she exhaled with disappointment. Wherever she was, it was too far from her mate for him to hear her call in his mind. Even if it seemed hopeless, she refused to die here in the clutches of Maverick. She needed to see her mate, touch her mate, and kiss her mate before her time ever expired.

"Are you okay?" Amber asked the moment Rita emerged from the bathroom. Rita figured her parents probably named her Amber from the amber color of her eyes and lightness of her skin, making her look like an amber gem.

"I'm strong," Rita replied. She got on the large bed with the three young wolves.

"I may be hurting, but as long as I remember that I'm strong, then I will be okay. Same thing goes for you three."

"But we're not strong." Maya quipped.

"The three of us shifted for the second time only days ago, and thanks to these silver cuffs we sort of have control of our wolves, but who's the say the moment we can finally shift we won't lose all control?" Maya's deep brown eyes and bronze skin made her look like she was carved from Egyptian stone.

"I agree with Maya," Amber said. Rita looked over at Brandy. She seemed the eldest of the three, but that was simply in her features. The only thing different about her was the fact that she was growing sister locks, but they were short and sprouted in all different directions whereas the other two had a head of curly, wild, untamed hair. Her lips were naturally plump, and her cheekbones were high giving her a mature look.

"I don't agree," Brandy said. "Yeah, we're young shifters, but that doesn't mean we have to be weak, and maybe we don't have control of our wolves, but that still doesn't mean we should be held here against our will, and look at these outfits. It's obvious they want to make us their fuck toys." All three wolves shivered.

"So gross," Maya stated.

"You don't have to wear those outfits," Rita said.

"I'd rather walk naked than to wear it. Lingerie gives males pleasure and shows submission, and as wolves, we're naked all the time, that's why they want us to wear those shits." After looking at each other, the three of them took off the outfits.

"You're mated?" Brandy asked pointing to Jayce's marks.

"Yes and no. We marked each other, but we didn't completely finish the bond."

"How come?" Maya asked.

"Complications." Rita sighed. "But I care very much for him."

"I can't wait to find my mate," Amber commented.

"Excuse me for being in your business and all, but once you shifted and went into heat who took care of you during the cycle?"

"One of the guys in my pack I like took care of mine," Maya said.

"The son of the Alpha did mine." Amber added.

"Same thing as Maya," Brandy said.

"Are you asking because they want us to be their fuck toys?" Amber asked. Rita nodded. The four of them went quiet. Rita could sense their vulnerabilities and fear. In response, she pushed positivity out towards them. At the same time, the three of them looked up at her and smiled.

"Tell us about your mate," Brandy said. Rita smiled when she thought about Jayce.

"He's a hardworking wolf, but the moment he gets around his friends, he becomes this laid-back man that plays teenage pranks on people and shit." Rita shook her head.

"I wanna see how he looks." Amber pouted. Maya quickly hopped off the bed. She searched the room until she found a large writing pad and a pen. She hopped back onto the bed.

"Describe him," Maya said.

"What are you doing?" Rita asked.

"You'll see! Just describe him." Shrugging, Rita gave Maya a deep description of what her mate looked like. Slowly on the pad, a hand-drawn image of Jayce appeared. Rita was taken aback by her talent in being able to just draw someone like that. It took her a whole hour with Rita correcting her on some of his attributes, but when she was done, she had it in the bag.

"Damn, Rita, your mate is kinda sexy," Amber said.

"Kinda?" Rita asked taking the paper from Maya. "He is sexy." She smiled.

"So, I guess you need to get out of here in one piece to get back to that sexy ass man," Brandy commented. Rita smirked and looked at the drawing. She drew her finger along the lines and imagined she was touching him.

"We're all gonna make it out of here," Rita said. "Don't worry about that." Nodding in response, the girls got comfortable on the large bed as fatigue consumed them. Once they'd drifted off to sleep, Rita crawled out of the bed. She went to the window hoping to see something outside to tell her where she was, but there was nothing but high trees and the sound and smell of water. Still, she took a deep breath and closed her eyes with the image of what was outside the window etched in her mind. She wasn't fully bonded to Jayce, but if he was close, she could project into his mind, but because she shared a blood vow with Kellan, and now Bliss, because of the mating, she could project into their minds no matter their distance.

She felt them deep in her core, and surely she knew they could feel her and the pain she was inflicted. She showed them the image knowing they would see it but not be able to speak to her. The image would come as almost like a flashback or a memory, something residual just like how they felt her pain. The silver cuffs weakened her ability to project too long, and after a moment, she was slumped over with exhaustion. Leaving the window, she climbed back into the bed with the three young wolves. She clutched onto the drawing of Jayce and prayed that her projection was enough for her pack mates to piece together where she was being kept.

Chapter Four

Kellan walked around Jayce in his wolf form panting. They were both out of breath and worn out from tearing each other apart. Bliss had long shifted back to human, but Jayce was still out of control, not able to calm his wolf down. While Kellan fought his friend, Tristan had scooped Bliss up and taken her away to safety. It had almost been thirty minutes of straight fighting, and Kellan was tired. The only reason why none of them could beat each other was because they all grew up training together. They knew too much about the other to lose a fight, but at the moment, Jayce was down, and Kellan's wolf felt satisfied that he whooped Jayce's ass enough for trying to attack his mate again.

Jaxson came into the cavern with clothes for both Jayce and Kellan. He bowed his head to his Alpha and backed away. Kellan shifted and snatched up the jeans and got dressed. Jayce shifted back moments later, still laying on the ground. He groaned as the claw marks Kellan left slowly healed. When he was able to, he got up and took the other pair of jeans and slowly dressed.

"Where's Bliss?" Jayce asked, worry dripping down his voice.

"She's back in-"

"Shut up." Kellan snapped at Jaxson. "You don't give reports on my mate." Jaxson nodded and backed up. He should have known better than that.

"As long as I didn't hurt her...I-"

"As long as you didn't hurt her?" Kellan gasped. "Are you out of your fucking mind?" Jayce stayed quiet.

"I'm prepared to help you get through the loss of Rita right now, but what I won't accept is my mate or anyone else in the pack getting hurt for your lack of control, and I'm supposed to be the level-headed one Jayce, but I swear to God you attack Bliss again I will kill you."

"I'm not attacking her on purpose." Jayce finally spoke. "But I will accept my punishment for it."

"Report back here tomorrow at nightfall for the punishment. Jaxson is going to shadow you for the rest of the night. Stay away from the she-wolves." Kellan ordered.

"I need to apologize to Bliss," Jayce said. "I owe her that much."

"Unfortunately, you've lost the privilege of saying shit to any of the she-wolves. Because you're my brother, Jayce, I want you to understand that I'm not just being a dick by keeping you away from them, because if you lose control, there is little I can do to fight my urge to protect the women. Any other man would have been dead for what you did to Bliss, and if you'd have done it to Gemma, I wouldn't be able to stop Tristan from getting at you. We know you can't control it, and we want Rita back as much as you do, but I can't battle against unpredictability."

Jayce felt alienated from his pack, but he couldn't blame Kellan for his verdict. Jayce was out of control, and without even realizing it until it was too late, he could have seriously hurt Bliss, but hearing his mate was in pain, Jayce couldn't handle it.

"What could they have been doing to her?" Jayce asked speaking of Rita. Kellan knew by the residual pain what might have been happening, but he wasn't going to tell Jayce that.

"Remember who Rita is," Kellan said.

"She's no weak wolf. She was an Omega for years before she found us. Don't take that lightly." Jayce was quiet as the image of Rita came into his mind.

"Is she still in pain?" Jayce asked.

"No, she's-" Kellan stumbled on his words as an image that wasn't his sparked in his mind. It stayed for only a moment before tinkering out. Jayce looked at him.

"What?"

"Nothing," Kellan said.

"I'll be around." He turned and left the cavern swiftly. No doubt the image had to do with Rita, but he couldn't trust Jayce with any information, not when he was this out of control.

Kellan walked the tunnels until he got to the large room he shared with Bliss. She was sitting on the bed with her knees against her chest. When he came into the room, she picked her head up.

"Why'd you put that image in my head?" she asked.

"That wasn't me," Kellan said.

"Rita?" Bliss asked. Kellan nodded. Bliss made a face and looked away.

"What?" He quizzed.

"It just feels like I've seen those treetops before, but I don't know."

"Sometimes with projection we take on what the person who's projecting may feel. Sometimes it's hard to separate our feelings from the ones being projected onto us." Bliss sighed hard and flopped back on the bed.

"How's Jayce?"

"He's fine."

"You didn't hurt him, did you?"

"Bliss, he was going to attack you." Bliss sat up and looked at him.

"I know what he did, but it's not his fault," Bliss said.

"I feel so bad for him. I'm responsible for Rita being taken."

"No, you're not," Kellan said. He got into the bed with her and put his arms around her. He kissed her temple trying to soothe her wolf. He hated when she felt like this.

"What are we going to do?" she asked.

"I feel so guilty being at your side and knowing that he doesn't have Rita at his side. Her, Kyra, and Gemma, they're my sisters. I can't have anything happening to any of them."

"I can't either, and I'll do what I need to do to protect anyone in this pack. I'm just upset that Maverick got the better of me in the way he did."

"We just have to commit to finding Rita and dealing with Maverick when the time is right."

"Based off what I saw in the projection, I'll head a search tomorrow morning. He could literally be anywhere. That's what scares me." Bliss rubbed his chest to calm his beast.

"Either way, we will not fail on this. I refuse to."
Kellan kissed his mate on the mouth before they eventually
drifted off to sleep.

When the sun rose the next day, Kellan was greeted
with breakfast by his packmates. In dreary times like this, the
table was quiet as everyone ate. It was hard to be happy or to
even crack jokes when you were missing a pack member.
Truthfully, they were missing not only Rita but Jayce. With
his control problems, he was in his room waiting until
everyone else ate before he came to eat anything.

"I'm gonna bring Jayce something to eat." Gemma
offered. Tristan grabbed Gemma by the elbow and pulled her
back before she got to walk anywhere.

"I don't think so," Tristan stated. Gemma huffed.

"Kellan," she said evenly. "Please tell your wolf to
take his hands off me."

"Really?" Tristan asked.

"Let her go, Tristan." Kellan ordered. Tristan let
Gemma go reluctantly. "But Tristan is also right. You can't
be near Jayce at the moment."

"He's still part of the pack, you know. We can't just alienate him." Her eyes gleamed into her wolf eyes in her anger and agitation. With her poor control, it wasn't unusual for her wolf to be sparked when she was passionate about something. Kellan sat back and pulsed his Alpha vibe at her. Her eyes returned to human immediately.

"Sorry," she whispered.

"No worries. We're not alienating Jayce. I just need to make sure everyone else is safe."

"You seem to be paying Jayce extra attention." Tristan accused. "Newsflash, he has a mate."

"Newsflash!" Gemma snapped at him. "So do you!" She bared her canines and growled. Tristan got in her face.

"Yeah? Whatcha' gonna do, huh?" he challenged her.

"Whoa!" Bliss stood and got in between them. She pushed Tristan back and gave Gemma a stern look.

"We have bigger problems than this right now. Our pack needs to be strong. We can't handle everyone falling apart. Tristan, you need to tone it down on the dickheadedness, and Gemma, you need to hold onto your wolf a little bit better. Men can be dicks. Doesn't mean you should stoop down to their level. Got it?" Gemma and Tristan just kept glaring at each other.

"Now, we're gonna go for a pack run like we've been doing every morning, and I don't wanna hear no more of this bickering and shit. Tristan, if you have a problem with how she cares for Jayce, then there's an easy solution." Bliss gave them both menacing looks before walking away. Kellan smirked at how his mate handled the pack in a position where she had no experience as an Alpha, but she was doing an amazing job. Kellan kissed her on the cheek as she walked by.

"Meet me outside the cave," Kellan said as he headed into one of the tunnel openings going to Jayce's bedroom. When he approached the door, it was already open, and Jaxson and Jayce inside. They were playing cards on the desk with a pile of money in between them.

"Fuck, I bust." Jaxson grunted as he slammed his cards down.

"Twenty-one," Jayce smiled. He scooped the money from the table and began counting it. Both the wolves looked up when Kellan entered.

"Pack run," he said. Jaxson got up.

"You couldn't come ten minutes earlier before I lost fifty bucks to this chump?" Jaxson asked.

"Not my fault you decided to play with him. We all know for some reason his ass never loses." Jaxson smirked as he walked out the room rolling his neck. Jayce stayed where he was.

"I said we're going for a pack run," Kellan said.

"I know what you said. Didn't know I was invited."

"Are you not part of the pack?" Jayce looked at his friend and smiled grimly. Kellan noticed the large holes in the side of the stone walls.

"You'd better fix this up before Rita gets back. I doubt she'd think holes in the wall would be decorative."

"She'd hate it." Jayce chuckled.

"She's never really seen that side of me. I threatened a wolf that tried to touch her in the pack before, but it didn't turn physical."

"Where mates are concerned, there's always something to be learned." Jayce nodded.

"Let's go. You can use the run." Jayce followed Kellan out of the room and all the way back to the front of the cave. Once they exited, Kellan used his palm print to close the metal door behind him. Like he'd asked, the pack was waiting for him outside of the cave. When Jayce emerged, everyone greeted him. Gemma squealed and gave him a hug, happy to see him. Not wanting to wait until Gemma was finished, Kyra and Bliss hugged Jayce at the same time. Jayce laughed and embraced his female pack members. After the turmoil he'd been experiencing, it was nice to still be accepted amongst the pack.

"Alright break it up," Kellan said pulling Bliss back.

"My wolf can't take it anymore." Bliss giggled and kissed her mate. Gemma and Kyra pulled back then walked with their Alpha female towards the woods. The men followed them, and walking behind the females, something flared in his chest. He wasn't sure what it was, but he just knew that his pack was going to be a force to reckon with, and all at once they all shifted, giving power to their beasts to run freely in the woods.

Chapter Five

"Wake up." Rory grunted slamming open the door to the bedroom where they were keeping the four women. All four of them jumped up.

"Wash up and put the outfits on. Let's go." He left the room before any of them could say something to him.

Rita didn't know what was going to be planned for the day, but she was ready for it. The three young wolves were nervous, but Rita tried to send them as much strength as she could. Her wolf was pacing back and forth, the silver cuffs making the animal extremely uncomfortable. All Rita wanted to do was shift, and that's what hurt the most.

"Don't put that on." Rita ordered once Amber was going for the lingerie. Amber put the flimsy material down. Rory came back into the room with a scowl on his face.

"Why aren't you dressed?" He grunted.

"We don't have any clothes, and we're not wearing the lingerie." Rory shook his head and chuckled.

"You must not realize where the hell you are," he said. He went quiet. "Maverick will be here in a moment." Rita sent confidence to the young wolves who began to shake with nervousness. Even though Rita wasn't showing her nervousness, she knew that by the sound of Maverick pounding through the house, he wasn't happy.

"What the fuck is going on?" He growled.

"They won't get dressed." Rory sighed.

"Put on the outfits." Maverick ordered.

"No," Rita replied.

"Do as I say and convince the young ones to do the same, or else you'll be spending more time in that room with my strap, Rita. What's your choice?" Rita came forward with her arms crossed.

"We need proper clothes," Rita said.

"Give them shirts." Maverick told Rory. Rita thought she won that battle, but Maverick reached forward and grabbed her by the hair. He yanked on her sister locs and pulled her towards him.

"No!" Amber gasped trying to reach for Rita, but Maverick pushed her down to the ground.

"It'll be alright!" Rita shouted trying to show the girls she would be fine. But she read on their faces that they knew nothing good would come of this. Maverick proceeded to drag Rita out of the room and down the hall. He brought her back to the darkroom where he'd tortured her the first time. He whipped her back and forth, yanking at her hair like he wanted to rip her locks from her scalp. Her momentum suddenly stopped when he landed his fist to her face. Rita was knocked back and onto the ground hard.

"I told you not to fuck with me, Rita." He snarled kicking her while she was on the ground.

"Here I have three young wolves, and you talkin' and movin' like you're the one runnin' shit. I'm not about to let you make me look like some type of pussy." Rita looked up at him from the ground.

"What you think they already look at you like?" She snarled. "You've kidnapped them and put your hands on female wolves. Only another bitch would respect you!"

"I'm gonna fuck you up, Rita!" he shouted marching towards her. In all his anger, Rita knew she couldn't best him, not with his strength, but remembering all that Jaxson taught her, she knew that if she was going to defend herself, it wasn't going to be with her own strength, so as he marched towards her, she used his momentum and kicked against his ankles. He fell forward, but his reflexes allowed him to catch himself. The attempt to get him off his feet angered him even more. He grabbed her by the neck in a chokehold. He held her high while squeezing her larynx. Even in this position, Rita still fought. Since he wanted to hold her in the air, she used that against him. Swinging her leg, she kicked him in the balls as hard as she could making sure to catch him with the silver cuff around her ankle. He dropped her immediately and howled out in pain. Rita fell with a hard thud, but she forced herself to get up before Maverick did. He had dropped to his knees holding his balls and that was the perfect position. On his knees, he was the perfect height for the roundhouse kick that she delivered to the side of his head.

"Fuck! You little bitch!" he yelled trying to grab onto her. Rita jumped out from his reach and used the heel of her foot to kick him dead in the face. His nose crushed under the force.

"How does it feel for a woman to finally fight back, huh?" Rita snapped. He grabbed for her again, and Rita was quick to dodge him before kicking him in the head again. If she had the use of her claws, she would be clawing his eyes out right at that moment, but since she didn't have her claws, she kept kicking him in the head hoping to knock him out. Her ability to fight back infuriated him. Maverick let out a deep growl before launching himself at her. He moved faster than she anticipated, knocking her down. He tried to grab for her neck again to choke her, but Rita learned this time. She grabbed onto his wrist then picked her legs up and wrapped them around his arm, hooking her ankles at his shoulders. She held tight and yanked hard on his arm putting him in and arm bar.

"BITCH!" He picked her up and tried to shake her off his arm, but Rita held tight. She was going to break his arm if she had to. She knew she could if she just held on, but with his other fist, he was jabbing punches to her side and face. Closing her eyes, Rita saw the fierceness in the eyes of her mate, and it gave her power enough to know that her strength wasn't all physicality, so she held on and kept yanking on his arm trying to tear it from the socket.

The door to the room burst open. Out of the corner of her eye, she saw Levi charging towards her. Rita gritted her teeth and yanked as hard as she could on Maverick's arm, but it didn't break in time before Levi was pulling at her hair. No matter how tight she was holding on, it still wasn't tight enough to combat both Maverick and another wolf who was yanking at her. Levi shook her loose and tossed her clear across the room. Her back hit the wall he threw her towards before she fell to a heap on the ground.

"What the fuck took you so long?" Maverick growled at Levi. "I been callin' you!"

"We have three other wolves, Maverick. I thought you could handle her." Maverick got in Levi's face.

"Don't get slick." He sneered. "Unless you wanna die like all the others will." Levi kept quiet.

"That's what I fucking thought." Maverick spat. He stormed past Levi and snatched up the whip he used on Rita the night before. Rita saw the reason her wounds hadn't healed from the beating. The tips of the whip were adorned by silver spikes, and that's all Rita could pay attention to as he slinked his slimy ass towards her.

"I had plans for us, Rita," he said. "You, me, and Bliss, the three of us would be the most amazing dynamic. Both of you pregnant with my pups, I'd be the most feared Alpha, but this little stunt you pulled." He rolled his shoulder.

"You're on too high of a horse, and it's clear I have to knock you down a bit."

"Beat me all you fucking want to." Rita gritted. "Still doesn't change the fact that you're a little bitch." Maverick's lips curled up in his anger. He raised the whip and brought it down hard against her skin. Rita closed her eyes and gritted her teeth against the pain. Even as tears clouded behind her closed lids, she refused to let them fall. That would give Maverick too much pleasure, and as the silver cut through her skin and scarred her even more, Rita thought of her Alphas again and used the strength from their vows to power her through another beating.

****

Kellan stopped walking sharply as the pain of what Rita was experiencing cut through him again. It felt like he was receiving sharp lashes to every part of his body. Immediately, Kellan sought out Bliss. She'd stopped walking also and was trying to maintain a steady breath to keep her wolf under control.

It's okay to shift, Kellan said in her mind. If she shifted before the pain was unbearable, then she wouldn't have to go through a forceful shift. The pack had just come back from their pack run, and though they were back in the cave, he would rather Bliss shift to not lose control. Bliss came up to him, her eyes flashing wolf.

"Help me control it," she said.

"If Rita is experiencing this pain, then I don't wanna run from it by shifting, but I want to have control like you do." Kellan kissed his mate on the forehead.

Tristan, watch over Jayce, please. Jaxson, I need you to get something for his punishment later. Gemma and Kyra, don't go anywhere near Jayce. Leave him be. Kellan spoke into the minds of his pack members as he led his mate to their bedroom. By the time they reached the room, Bliss was breathing hoarsely.

"I don't understand. I thought I had control when I was able to shift back and forth with no problem," she said.

"It's not just about shifting though. Sometimes, your wolf just wants control, and you have to be the one to make sure you stay in control. Naturally, feeling pain, your wolf will try and protect you from that, and she'll forcefully bring herself out whether you want her to or not. If you want to stay in control, you have to convince her that you can protect yourself at the moment." Bliss looked at him with her canines falling from her mouth.

"Alpha. Beta. Omega," Kellan said to her.

"Repeat it."

"Alpha. Beta. Omega." Bliss breathed.

"Close your eyes. Breathe in like you're about to fill a balloon up with air, and then let it out slowly. Then say the words, but when you say it, I need you to say it firmly and confidently." Bliss did as her mate asked. She took a deep breath, exhaled, then repeated the mantra.

"Alpha. Beta. Omega." She repeated it over and over. At first, there seemed to be no type of result, but in her mind, her wolf took a dominant stance, but as if sensing Bliss's confidence, she bowed and began to retreat. When Bliss opened her eyes, her canines had receded, and her eyes were back to normal.

"You did it." Kellan smiled. Bliss let out a sigh.

"Thanks for teaching me." Kellan leaned over and kissed her softly on the lips. "She was in pain again."

"Yeah, but did you feel anything behind the pain?" Kellan asked. Bliss shook her head. She was too focused on trying to control her wolf to feel anything else.

"She was in pain, I felt that clearly, but there was also this kind of fight there, like she wasn't weak. She's fighting, and though she's hurting, I have confidence that she'll know how to keep herself alive before we can find her."

"I read this book where it says that being an Alpha, you can find anyone of your packmates by just their howl," Bliss said.

"Well, it's kind of true, but also not all the way true. If Rita howled, I'd be able to find her, but realistically, distance comes into play. If she's one hundred miles away, I doubt I would hear her if she howled, and then there's the fact that I can only find her location if she howled as a wolf or in between her shift into a wolf. If she's human, I wouldn't hear her."

"Does she know this?"

"Yeah, she does." Kellan sighed.

"Which means if she hasn't howled, it's because she can't." Kellan shook his head.

"I've got some thinking to do," he said. He kissed Bliss again before leaving the room. He headed out of the cave entirely so he could figure out how to lead his pack on a rescue mission for one of their pack mates.

By nightfall, the pack was having another meeting to assess the situation further. Jayce and Tristan were in the meeting room first followed by Bliss, Kellan, and Jaxson. For this meeting, Kellan permitted Gemma and Kyra in on the meeting because he needed every ounce of help he could get.

"Any updates?" Kellan asked.

"Still no response from the other pack," Jayce replied. Kellan looked at Gemma.

"Gemma, the pack your parents moved to haven't been responding at our attempts at communication. We've also called your parents and received nothing from them." Gemma looked around the room.

"They told me they were hiding out with their new Alpha. Someone attacked the pack and sent them running. They called me to tell me what happened. They think their pack is being hunted. They're safe now but refuses to get in touch with anyone because they don't want anyone else targeted either."

"Why didn't you report that to us?" Kellan asked.

"Because we have to find Rita and I didn't want to add any more issues to the pot. My parents are fine that's all I need to hear."

"So on top of Maverick being out there; someone else is targeting packs? I mean the pack I left your parents with Gemma are as platonic as you can get. No one should be out to hunt them down. They're not threatening in the least bit," Jayce spoke up.

"Well the sooner we find Rita, the sooner we can go and help packs like that," Bliss said.

"I've been thinking," Jaxson said. "Bliss you know the human side of Maverick. Maybe that can help us determine where he might be."

"That's true, but he was also able to hide the fact that he was a shifter to me. And much of the human things he did I wasn't aware of. I know he sells and buys businesses. That's how he was in partnership with my father."

"So he owns businesses?" Jayce asked.

"Yes. I don't know about all of them. But he owns a restaurant, a lounge and a real estate company."

"What if he's using those businesses as a front of his shifter activity. Maybe he's holed up in one of those buildings knowing we'd never go into the human world looking for him," Jaxson added.

"That should be our next move. Bliss can lead us to wherever his businesses are, and we can tear the damn place up looking for Rita," Jayce said. Kellan was quiet. He didn't like the idea of Bliss being put in the forefront of this battle like that. After Rita being taken he could ill afford for any of his female wolves to be put in that predicament again.

"Relax," Kellan said. "We're not gonna make any hasty decisions. I do however think that none of the female wolves should be accompanying us on any of these missions. From what he said about Rita as they took her it's pretty clear that the females are the target. I'm not losing another wolf to him."

"I agree," Tristan said. "They should stay in the cave where they're protected."

"Of course you say that," Bliss mumbled. "You're like some kind of misogynist, male chauvinist cult leader or something." Tristan gasped.

"You'd use those words against me when I just want our females to be protected?" Tristan asked.

"You wanna clock us wherever we go!" Bliss snapped. "And Kellan if I wanna help lead the charge against Maverick then I should have the right to do so. I am the alpha too you know."

"That doesn't make me a chauvinist," Tristan growled.

"Bliss," Kellan warned.

"Don't warn me," Bliss snapped. "Warn him! Where do the both of you get the idea that the she-wolves don't want to be involved? Where do you even get the idea that you can tell us not to be involved without even giving us a chance to voice our own opinions about what we want to do?"

"She's right! I want to be there to rescue Rita too. She's our sister. You men can't just tell us to fall back and not expect us to fight," Gemma spoke up.

"Oh give me a goddamn break Gemma," Tristan said. "What possible good can you do us in a damn fight? You can't even control your damn wolf."

"And that's what makes me a good fighter! I don't see why I have to explain myself to you anyways. You're not my damn alpha."

"Can we stop this fighting," Kyra shouted. "It's not getting us nowhere."

"Kyra is right!" Jayce said. "We need to find my mate. That's all."

"So we're helping," Bliss said. "I know where the locations are. I can take you to them."

"You're not taking us there," Kellan said sternly. "You and the she-wolves will stay behind."

"We won't stay behind!" Bliss snapped. "I can't believe my mate is just as chauvinistic as Tristan."

"Stop calling me that!" Tristan yelled banging his fist on the table.

"It's what you are," Bliss mumbled surprised he raised his voice at her.

"What I am is a wolf who doesn't want to see the females of his pack get hurt or snatched up by some maniac. Maverick is no laughing matter, and we need to face the fact that he bested us the last time we confronted him! I'm not gonna go up against those odds again cause I refuse to be beaten by him! Bliss, you can do whatever you want if Kellan allows it but Gemma you're not gonna be involved in this fight. You can help us strategizing, but there will be no physicality from you. Especially fighting!"

"You don't have any right to tell her what she can and cannot do," Bliss spoke up for Gemma.

"I know you think I'm discriminating and I'm this pig, but that's my mate," Tristan said pointing to Gemma.

"Whether I want to accept it or not; the universe gave her to me. I may be in denial about what I want right now, but one things for damn sure I'm not being a dick because I have something against women. I'm this way because I'm not as strong as Jayce. I can't have my mate at the mercy of a lunatic and not go completely rogue." Tristan looked directly at Gemma before getting up and stomping out of the room. Gemma looked around the room for a moment before she cursed and got up to run after Tristan.

"Wait!" Gemma called after him. He wasn't slowing down or stopping, so Gemma ran up to him and jumped onto his back.

"Stop," She breathed into his ear. "Talk to me." He stopped walking and sighed. Gemma slid down his back and stood in front of him.

"What?" he asked.

"I just-you haven't claimed me like that since we knew we were mates. I thought you didn't give a fuck about me."

"I never said I didn't care about you."

"Your actions were pretty much doing all the talking." Tristan looked down at her plump lips. He grasped her by the side of the neck and pulled her into him. For a while, he'd been wondering what her lips tasted like. So when he pecked her softness both he and his wolf were more than elated. Her cinnamon scent invaded his senses and drowned him in its sweetness. Sighing he deepened the kiss by piercing her mouth with his tongue. Her inexperience of kissing showed in the tentative way she kissed him back, but it almost didn't matter. His arousal made him stiff in his jeans as he held his young mate and kissed her inexperienced mouth. He pulled away from her slowly as thoughts about doing much more to her raged through his mind. Gemma's chest was rising and falling heavily as she looked into her mate's eyes. Both of them had glowing eyes.

"I care about you," He whispered. "More than you can even imagine. And I won't see you hurt." He pecked her mouth one last time before he backed away from her and the continued to walk away. Gemma stood there dumbfounded for a moment with her fingertips against her lips. Her first kiss. She knew all about fairytales and true love and all that, and as a wolf, she believed in true love because there was always that one wolf on the earth that was made for you. She imagined what her first kiss would feel like and her imagination didn't do anything for the real thing. For the first time, her wolf wasn't pushing to gain control of her. She was laying down wither tail wagging and her tongue lolling out. She was more than relieved that her wolf was relaxed. But then she was concerned because her wolf needed its mate to be calm.

Gemma walked back to the meeting room slowly, still touching her lips. When she entered the room, everyone was talking over each other trying to come to a solution. Jayce was the only quiet one. Gemma guessed that was so because his eyes were turned wolf and he was battling for control of his animal. When her pack mates spotted her, the talking stopped. Everyone looked at her.

"We'll take a back seat," Gemma said.

"What?!" Bliss gasped.

"I thought you wanted to fight!"

"I do," Gemma confessed.

"But there's more to fighting than throwing fists. Strategizing and formulating plans is a very important part of any fight we'll have with Maverick. I can understand why Tristan and Kellan feel the way they do."

"You let that chauvi-"

"Stop," Gemma said lightly. "You're my alpha female Bliss, and I respect you. But I'm going to insist you stop disrespecting my mate by calling him that. I won't take too kindly to it if you do it again." She gave Bliss a piercing stare before smiling at her. Bliss nodded. She had nothing to do but respect Gemma for speaking up for her mate.

"Sorry," Bliss said. "He does deserve my respect." Bliss turned to Kellan.

"I'll give you as much information as I can to help find Rita. We'll be here to support you however you may need us." Kellan kissed his mate.

"Meeting adjourned," he declared. He looked at Jayce.

"It's time," he said. Jayce grunted and headed out of the room.

"Time for what?" Bliss asked. Kellan only kissed her again before leaving the room. Jaxson followed out behind him leaving the females alone.

"I guess I should apologize to Tristan," Bliss said to Gemma. "I just got so heated about being left out."

"I don't blame you. But they have a point. What if one of us were to get snatched? Or something even worse were to happen?"

"All I know is we'll get Rita back, and we'll have our chance to get back at Maverick," Kyra spoke up.

"Even if we can't use muscle right now, we can use our brains. And Maverick is a dumb muthafucker. He can't get too far without us catching his ass."

"True that," Bliss said. She looked at Gemma who was spaced out. "Gem," she called. Gemma snapped up from her daze.

"Did you say something?" she asked.

"Damn girl, what the hell you thinking about so hard?" Kyra asked. She leaned over and sniffed Gemma. "Ew girl! Are you horny?!"

"No!" Gemma shrieked. But then her cheeks tinted with blush.

"Yes, you are!" Kyra laughed. "I thought you said sex was a no go for you since you experienced how painful going into heat was?"

"Sex was a no go for me," Gemma said. "I didn't even want to think about being intimate ever again."

"So what happened?" Bliss asked.

"I got kissed for the first time." Gemma touched her lips again as Bliss and Kyra smiled.

"No wonder you came up in here defending him the way you did. Please, tell us more." Bliss took Gemma by the arm and began leading her out with Kyra following next to them.

Chapter Six

Down the in the cellar, Kellan, Tristan, and Jaxon were standing in a semi-circle around Jayce. Being Beta, Jayce had been part of many a punishments, but he couldn't say he was ever the one being punished. He followed pack rules to a tee, but his behavior regarding his alpha female couldn't be ignored despite whatever he was going through. No matter the case he wasn't going to make an excuse or back down from a punishment. When rules were broken in the pack, there were repercussions.

"You are being reprimanded on counts of losing control of your wolf and in doing so launching an attack on your alpha female. Whether intentional or not, pack rules forbid attacks on another pack member without reasonable cause. You do however have the right to defend yourself against a pack member if you have been attacked. You also, however, have the right to dispute these accusations brought against you."

"No dispute," Jayce said. "I take full responsibility for my actions and accept the punishment." Kellan looked at him for a while contemplating.

"Look, I know there's rules against this shit, but no matter how upset I am for the way you attacked Bliss I can't punish you. Not when all this is because I let our enemy snatch up your mate."

"It doesn't matter the circumstance," Jayce said. "The rules are the rules." Kellan nodded in respect. Jaxson stepped forward with silver shackles in his hands. It was the same silver shackles that his father had used for certain punishments when he was alpha. Since Maverick was gone from the territory, they were free to go back and collect more things to bring back to their new home. Kellan never imagined that he would use the same silver shackles that his father had.

"Because of your lack of control, it seems fit to restrict your ability to shift for Twenty-Four hours," Kellan said. Jayce held his hands out and allowed Kellan to place the shackles around his wrists. Jayce fell to his knees. The silver touching his skin suffocated his shifter power. He gritted his teeth and groaned as his wolf launched itself at the magical barrier that should have allowed him to trade places with Jayce. The wolf continued to fight against the barrier until he was too weak. He flopped down panting hard. Jayce was breathing hoarsely. It may have seemed that simply wearing silver shackles was an easy punishment, but denying a shifter the ability to shift was the ultimate imprisonment. And it wasn't to be taken lightly.

"Twenty-Four hours. I would hope that after your time has passed, you would have found a coping mechanism to ensure that you can keep control of your wolf. I expect you spend your time in solitude." Kellan nodded at Jayce before backing away.

"Tristan, Jaxson, let's go," he ordered. Without another word, the alpha and his enforcers left their beta alone for his punishment. Even though Kellan kept a tough face, he hated the idea that he went through with punishing someone. When his father passed down punishments, Kellan was always the one protesting and advocating against the punishment. But being alpha was going to open him up to things he never imagined he would be doing.

In their bedroom, Bliss was freshly showered; rubbing her skin with shea butter. She was humming along to a song playing on their portable speaker. She slipped into a short silk nightgown and got into bed.

"Are you alright?" She asked him.

"Yup," he replied shortly. Of course, she gave him a look as he sat on the edge of the bed.

"What's wrong with Jayce?" she questioned. "I feel something is wrong through your bond with him."

"Nothing's wrong with him."

"After the meeting, you told him it was time. What were you talking about?"

"He's being punished for attacking you."

"Seriously?" Bliss asked. "Punished how?"

"That's just the way of packs Bliss. Breaking rules has repercussions."

"His mate had been taken! He wouldn't be acting that way if Rita was here."

"I know that Bliss. I was going to punish him at first. And then I changed my mind, but he refused it. He wanted the punishment, so I did what I had to do." Bliss shook her head. She got out of bed and pulled on a long robe.

"Where are you going?" Kellan asked.

"To talk to Jayce."

"Bliss-"

"Just leave me be Kellan. I wanna talk to him and I will." Kellan just shook his head and let her walk out of the room. He wasn't in the mood to fight anyway.

"You can't go in there," Jaxson said blocking the door to the cellar.

"Get out of my way," Bliss ordered. "I just wanna talk to him. And if you don't let me by, I'll be telling Kellan you're being mean to me." Jaxson crossed his arms.

"When are you going to stop using that on me?" he asked stepping to the side.

"Never," Bliss giggled. Jaxson conked her on the head lightly as she walked by him and into the cellar. Jayce looked up immediately. Bliss didn't know what to expect to see, but he was just sitting there Indian style, deep breathing.

"Hey Jayce," She smiled going over to him.

"Kellan let you down here?" he asked. Bliss scoffed.

"He knows if he doesn't give me what I want then I won't give him what he wants," she said.

"And I don't think he wants to deal with that," Jayce smirked.

"So I hear you're on some kind of punishment? But you look fine." Jayce held up his wrists showing her silver shackles.

"Silver is our kryptonite. I can't shift. It traps me, but I feel like it's what I need right now."

"Silver bullets," Bliss said.

"The only thing guaranteed to kill us. That plus wolfs bane." Jayce nodded.

"Why you gonna subject yourself to this? I don't like it not one bit," Bliss complained.

"Not tired of me attacking you?"

"The first time was my fault. I wanted to train with you. And if you ask me, this is all quite ironic. Using silver against our own kind. It's barbaric. And I don't think you deserve it no matter how often you attacked me."

"Says the woman coming from a human system that at one point legalized the sale and ownership of human beings with dark skin, but at the same time honors the right of a human being with pink skin." Bliss hummed.

"Right…." She sighed. "No one is perfect. How long you gonna be in those?"

"Twenty-Four hours," he replied. "It hurts to be sort of trapped, but then again my conscience can be relaxed knowing I can't lose control."

"Not being able to shift doesn't mean you won't lose control."

"Meaning?"

"You might be physically incapable of shifting and turning rogue, but your mind is still very functional. And being trapped the way you are will make you lose control of your mind instead of your body."

"You're almost too smart for your own good," Jayce sighed.

"What am I going to do? Until we get her back, I'm going to be a mess." Bliss wasn't sure if it would work or not, but when Kellan taught her that mantra, she realized how powerful it was.

"When you think about Rita, what's the one thing that you like the most about her?" Bliss asked him.

"Her slick ass mouth," he smiled.

"She's not afraid to say what she has to."

"I know you said the two of you had just met when you realized she was your mate. But what has been your fondest memory of her? Or something you'll never forget."

"It gets a little personal," Jayce said leaning back with his arms crossed.

"Cut the shit Jayce. You wanna learn to control your wolf without Rita or what?" Jayce rolled his eyes and sighed.

"I won't ever forget the first time we made love. Actually, I wouldn't even call it making love. We fucked each other because the both of us reached a point where we couldn't resist anymore. I wanted to mark her, so everyone knew she belonged to me. But even though we're mates, it takes a lot to give yourself over to someone. And she trusted me enough to give herself to me. And I won't ever forget how it felt to be one with her. I think part of my biggest issue with losing her is the fact that I had her. I had her, and I just-I just let her go."

"Don't think about what could have been Jayce. Think about what lays ahead for the two of you. Unfortunately, you fucked up already. No use in staying in your bag about it. Now is all about your future." Bliss stood and walked over to the entrance of the cellar.

"Give me the keys to the shackles," she said to Jaxson.

"Absolutely not. You crazy?"

"I'm not going to break his punishment I just want to try something. If I shout for help; get your ass in here quick." She smiled and took the keys from him. Jaxson sucked his teeth but let his alpha female do whatever she wanted.

"I'm gonna try something," Bliss said going back over to Jayce. She leaned over him with the key to the shackles.

"You trippin' right now?" Jayce asked.

"You know I don't like all this third degree. Just let me do what I'm doing." Jayce kept quiet as she removed the silver shackles from his wrist.

"I hope you know that undermining the final verdict or rule of the alpha is highly frowned upon," Jayce said.

"What's he going to do? Spank me?" Bliss shrugged.

"He might do more than that," he said. Bliss waved him off and got back to the task at hand.

"Do you know the alpha, beta, omega mantra?" she asked him.

"Of course I know it."

"Ever thought about using it when you've felt yourself losing control?" Jayce shook his head.

"Not until I was in control of my wolf after I hit puberty."

"Well, you ain't been in control of your wolf. So once you start losing yourself, I want you to use the mantra."

"I highly doubt it's going to work on me. My wolf is too old for that."

"I don't want you to just say it though. It might not work that way. As you say it, I want you to see her in your mind. See the way she smiles at you. Remember the way it felt to have her body. To know that she was giving herself to you as her mate. Think about her touch and think about her scent. And then make sure your wolf knows that you and her have a future together."

"Well, when I get to that bridge I will cross it."

"How 'bout now?"

"What?"

"I always think that sometimes if Kellan hadn't saved me, then he and Rita would have started a pack by themselves and had pups. After all, she was convinced you didn't want anything to do with her. And you haven't given her any reason to think otherwise either." Bliss backed up as Jayce's eyes went wolf and his breathing went hoarse.

"Are you trying to get yourself killed?" he asked intently.

"I'm just telling you I think your woman wants my mate instead of you. And you'd better find her before Kellan does or you don't stand a chance," she scoffed. Jayce felt his claws and canines elongate. When he let out a deep growl, Bliss continued to back up.

"Alpha. Beta. Omega," Bliss said to him firmly lacing her voice with the powers that made her an alpha wolf. If she hadn't, she doubted Jayce would even hear her. He stopped growling, but his glowing eyes never left her.

Jayce's wolf had its hackles up, ready attack the person responsible for even insinuating that Rita didn't belong to him. He would fight anyone ready to challenge his position as her mate. The wolf struggled against the power of his alpha, but he was still ready to attack. Jayce wouldn't forgive himself for attacking anyone in his pack again, so he had to try to reign the wolf in. Doing what Bliss suggested he forced himself to see Rita in his mind. What he brought forth was the first time he ever heard her voice in his head, and then the first time he saw her face when she'd shifted in his presence. He remembered how her scent has consumed him and when they locked stares it was as if the universe shifted under them. And even though it had been an adjustment to get used to the idea of having a mate but every time he saw her she smiled at him in a way that pumped life into his body as if she was the organ that gave him life. And he knew the moment he had her in his arms again she was going to give him that same smile. And he was going to come alive.

Alpha. Beta. Omega. He said the words in his head never letting go of the memory of his mate's smile, her scent, and after they'd shared bodies the first time, he knew she belonged to him. He repeated the mantra until his wolf began to slowly back away, nodding as if understanding there was no reason to panic. Their mate wasn't going anywhere.

Bliss exhaled loudly when Jayce's eye's returned to normal. His teeth slowly went back up into his mouth. Her heart had been beating a mile a minute waiting to see if he would pounce on her or if her plan worked.

"Thank goodness," She sighed. Jayce looked at her with a calm demeanor. She smiled at him as she crawled back towards him.

"So it worked," she said.

"So it did," he replied. She put the shackles back onto his wrist.

"I guess this means that you don't have to subject yourself to punishment because you think it'll help you control your wolf." She closed the shackles with a snap then rubbed his hands.

"Well since you'll be here for twenty-Four hours, you should keep practicing the mantra and your special thoughts of your mate." Bliss stood then leaned over and kissed Jayce on the cheek. He gave her a small smile and watched as she walked out of the cellar.

"Thanks, Bliss," he called out after her.

"Anytime."

Chapter Seven

Rita was on her hands and knees scrubbing the kitchen floor of Maverick's large house. The welts of pain she had from her beating earlier still throbbed all over her body proof that the silver in the whip was scarring her body. Maverick hadn't allowed her to shower after the beating, so she'd been walking around the house cleaning up after Hera and the other wolves with blood running down her naked body. She was being treated like the common housemaid but even worse than that.

"Yo make me something to eat," Rory ordered her coming into the kitchen. Rita stood from the floor trying to hide her grimace. She didn't want to show any kind of weakness to these chumps.

"Make yourself something to eat," She snapped at him. He gave her an evil grin and lifted the whip he had in his hand.

"Maverick says we're open to knocking you down a few pegs if your refuse to listen." Rita just shrugged.

"Give it your best shot." He lashed the whip out landing it between her breasts. Even though it burned she forced herself not to make any expression. Rory looked at her confused as to why she wasn't affected. Rita just walked by him giving him a glare. Of course, he couldn't just let her go, so he tried to grab her neck. She turned around sharply and grabbed his wrist twisting it until it snapped. With his wrist still in her hand, she picked her foot up and kicked him in the face.

"Don't fucking try me, Rory," she gritted. "Captive or not I'll kick your fucking ass." She pushed him to the ground and stomped on his nuts before continuing out of the kitchen.

"You. Come here," Maverick shouted from down the hall. She was hoping to retire back to the room with the girls instead of continuing this maid shit.

"What you want?" Rita asked looking at him.

"Just come the fuck here Rita." After rolling her eyes, Rita walked down the hall towards him. She looked around the house taking in her surroundings. Even if she could have refused cleaning and took the consequences for her refusal she didn't want to do that. Being their maid gave her access to knowing what the house looked like. If she knew where things were then making an escape was going to be a little bit easier. When she was in front of him, he grabbed her by the back of the neck and led her to a large master bedroom. Hera was sitting comfortably in the middle of the bed naked. Rita felt the pulses of a nearby heat cycle. She stopped in her tracks immediately.

"No," she said. "If she's in heat I don't wanna be in here!"

"Why?" Maverick questioned. "Because it'll trigger your heat cycle?"

"Why the fuck do you think Einstein!" Rita snapped at him. Maverick backhanded her.

"Watch your fucking mouth!" He walked over to Hera.

"I've decided to take matters into my own hands. Her heat cycle won't come along for who knows how long. I can't wait for her. You and the other wolves won't be in heating either. But thanks to human medicine I think I fixed that problem. I injected her with fertility medication which in facts seems to be triggering her heating cycle. If I can get her in heat then I can trigger the rest of you."

"Sick bastard," Rita shook her head.

"You'll get used to it," Maverick smiled.

"Now sit in the damn corner and watch daddy work." Rita made a face and kept standing as Maverick went to Hera and pulled her on all fours. She rolled her eyes and looked away as they started fucking. It was so unnatural to pump those damn human drugs into their bodies. Rita didn't think anything good was going to come out of it. And now she had to sit here and watch this freak show in front of her. She felt the oncoming of heat waves and just had to pray that she would have escaped by the time she would be affected by the heating cycle.

Rita felt herself gagging as Maverick grunted and shouted in pleasure from his release. Hera fell from all fours back onto the bed. The stench in the room was almost unbearable.

"Run her a bath and help her clean up," Maverick ordered Rita. Rita scrunched up her nose.

"She gonna need more than a bath for that stench," Rita said. "Can't imagine how you fuck it."

"At least my body is perfect," Hera snapped. "I don't have scars all over my damn body. And I don't think Jayce would appreciate a mate with such imperfections." Rita looked down at her body insecurity beginning consume her mind. Unlike all her other emotions Rita was unable to hide the fact that what Hera said did have an effect on her.

"And if you keep running your mouth I'll be giving you more scars to take back to your mate."

"So are you insinuating that I'll be returning to my pack?" Rita asked, deciding not to have Hera dwell on the fact that she managed to get Rita in her feelings.

"What?" Hera asked confused.

"You said I'll have more scars to take back to my mate. That means you're planning on letting me go. But Maverick here wants me to stay and have his pups, and he fully intends to kill Jayce. So me having scars and being unacceptable for my mate shouldn't even really matter should it? Unless she's calling the shots now Maverick and I am going to return to my pack?" Maverick stared coldly at Hera.

"See what happens when you run your fucking mouth? I told you she and the rest of the girls are having my pups. You don't get to decide shit about what goes on. And if she's having my damn pups, then she won't be going back to her damn mate. She'll be taking care of our damn offspring."

"I still don't see why you need the rest of them when you have me."

"I'm not going through this shit with you. Take ya ass on in the bathroom." Maverick waved her off ending the conversation. Hera huffed and marched to the connecting bathroom inside the room. Rita followed to continue being their maids. She turned on the water in the large jacuzzi tub and waited for it to fill up.

"He might wanna have pups with you, but don't get it twisted," Hera sneered at her.

"Get what twisted? That you're willingly fucking a psycho?"

"No! That I'm his alpha female and I'll be the one in charge here. Not you or any female he brings around."

"That's up for debate," Rita joked. She was only saying it to get under Hera's skin, but when she thought about it a plan formulated in her brain.

"Get in," Rita ordered once the water was ready. Hera sank into the tub, submerging herself completely to wet her hair before coming back to the surface and sitting down.

"Wash my hair," she ordered. What Rita wanted to do was rip Hera's hair from her scalp, but she simply gave the woman a fake smile and proceeded to wash her hair and then sponge her body down. Once that was done, Rita simply left the bathroom. She was already bathing a grown ass woman, and she was through pampering her. Back in the bedroom, Maverick was going through some papers. He didn't even look up at her, but Rita approached his desk.

"What?" he asked.

"So how come I'm not getting pampered by someone?" She questioned. He looked at her then.

"You talk back to me, and you tried to break my arm. Think you're getting any pampering?" Rita wasn't sure if her plan was going to work, but she decided if this conversation went well then the chances of Maverick falling for her plan would increase.

"So if I stopped all of that then I'd get pampered?" Maverick put his pen down and turned to look at her.

"I told you when you first arrived that I wasn't interested in treating my own kind like garbage. But you have been testing me, and therefore that's why you have been treated the way you have been."

"I just think if I'm going to have your pups too then I should get the same treatment that Hera is getting. And so should the other wolves."

"Oh, so you're saying you want to have my pups now huh? Just moment ago you were calling me names."

"I say all those things, and I fight because I don't want to seem weak."

"No one would have thought that of you," Maverick said. Rita shifted on her feet and lowered her head as if she appear shy.

"Do you, do you think I'm pretty?" she asked him. He seemed stunned by her question, and for the first time, Maverick had nothing to say for a moment. Rita used it to her advantage.

"I knew it. You don't think I'm pretty at all." She turned around as if to walk away but Maverick stood and grabbed her by the elbow and turned her back around.

"I didn't say you weren't pretty Rita," He said.

"When I took over Kameron's pack I wanted you as my woman, and you turned me down and ran away from me."

"Because you scared me! But if I'm here and this is the life that I'm going to be resorted to, then I at least want to feel wanted. Like you chose me to be here because you saw something in me not because I'm just another body. I may have run from you at first and given you hell since I've been here, but I haven't said that you aren't strong or handsome." She touched his chest feeling it rise and fall rapidly. Because of the silver cuffs, she couldn't hear his heartbeat.

"It's hard to believe you changed just like that. Now all of a sudden you want to be here?" Rita shrugged.

"Maybe I'm just accepting fate. It's not like my mate wants me anyway."

"And your alpha? You realize I'm going to kill him?"

"Maybe you don't have to. If I'm not showing him allegiance anymore, then he won't need to come and rescue me." Maverick looked at her deeply considering something. Hera emerged from the bathroom.

"We'll discuss this at another time," Maverick told her. To increase her chance of her plan working, she leaned forward and kissed him lightly. He jumped in surprise and looked at her. Rita looked away trying to appear embarrassed. She felt his eyes, but he didn't say anything to her about the kiss.

"Go on to bed Rita," He said.

"I'll see you in the morning." She nodded and hurried off. She knew the way to the room where she and the other wolves were staying, but the house was big enough to confuse her on what exactly was the front door. There was a door in the kitchen where she assumed either led to a garage or the outside. But that was all she knew.

She hurried to the bedroom and found the three wolves already inside. They had a plate of food on the night table stand for her.

"We were so worried about you," Maya said giving her the plate. Rita sat on the bed and began devouring the chicken and mac and cheese.

"Don't worry about me. He had me doing all these damn chores, but I got through it. What about you three?"

"Nothing. We stayed in here for most of the day."

"Look," Rita whispered. She was about to say her plan but decided against it. She couldn't take the chance that Maverick might hear her. Her powers may have been gone, but his wasn't. She reached for the notepad and scribbled on it.

I have a plan. Don't know if it'll work yet, but make sure to follow my lead. All three wolves read the note, and Amber who read it last tore it up to pieces.

"We'll go with whatever you say," Maya said.

"We trust you," Brandy smiled. Rita smiled at the wolves before all three of them hugged her tightly.

"Let's get some sleep," Rita said.

Chapter Eight

"RITA!" The shrill screaming of her name shocked Rita in awareness. She jumped up from the bed, rubbing sleep from her eyes. Rory was inside their room holding onto Amber. Maya and Brandy were holding onto her legs trying to keep Rory from taking her. It took Rita a moment to adjust to the chaos that was happening because of the wear down from the silver cuffs. She would continue to get weaker and weaker. But she finally got herself up to help the three wolves.

"What the hell are you doing?!" Rita screamed joining Brandy and Maya in trying to get Amber from his hold. His eyes shone wolf clearly, he was amped up about something. And even if it was three against one he was going to be stronger.

"Let her the fuck go," Rory snapped. "My wolf wants some action and one of y'all is coming with me whether you want to or not." Rita saw the fear in Amber's eyes at realizing what Rory wanted with her. But still, Rory out powered the three wolves. He snatched Amber away sending Rita, Maya, and Brandy flying. He ripped the t-shirt she was wearing off and clawed one of her breasts in his excitement. He popped the breast in mouth and sucked at her nipple. Amber screamed in disgust and fear. She looked at Rita with a desperate expression.

"Please don't let him," she begged. Rory began dragging her out of the room.

"WAIT!" Rita shouted. She got you and quickly took her t-shirt off.

"Leave her and take me." Rory paused and looked at Rita. Even though she had scars all over her body from her lashes, she was still incredibly beautiful. Her breasts were in perfect proportion to the swell of her hips and her ass. Amber was a young wolf, and he doubted she knew how to pleasure a grown wolf-like himself. But Rita, she dripped of sensuality. And after the way she'd been treating him, he figured he could teach her a lesson or two by beating the shit out of her pussy.

"Hey, if you wanna trade places with her that's on you. But letting me have you today don't mean you'll save her from another day," he said pushing Amber away from him.

"Now come here," he ordered. Amber crawled away as fast as she could. Rita helped her stand from the ground.

"Don't do it. There can be another way," she rushed out.

"No, there's no other way. He's gonna want what he wants no matter what. As long as you three are safe, then I'll be alright. Trust me." She ruffled Amber's hair before pushed her towards Brandy and Maya and walking to Rory. He grabbed her by the elbow and dragged her away.

"You're gonna regret this," he laughed. "I'm gonna fuck your shit until you can't even walk. Watch. I'm hard as a rock thinking about that shit."

"Where's Maverick?" Rita asked.

"He went out. Which means I have some free time." Rory led her down a hall she hadn't been in and into a room that was just as big as all the other rooms. But it was untidy like any male's room, so Rita figured it was where Rory stayed. He threw her against his bed and eagerly began to strip. Rita turned and looked at him. Thankfully he wasn't that ugly or else this would have been unbearable. And when he fisted his dick in his hand she tried not to gag. He was in no size comparison to Jayce thankfully so while he thought he was going to hurt her that might not be the case.

"Let me see what that mouth do," he ordered. He walked over to her and yanked her from the bed by the wrist forcing her to her knees. Rita paused with opening her mouth and clearly her indecision was too much for him to wait on. He held her at the cheeks with his hand, squeezing until her mouth was forced open.

"If you bite me I swear I'll kill you," he gritted. "I don't give a damn what Maverick wants to use you for." Rita snapped her eyes closed not wanting to even see what she was about to do. He pumped his tip against her lip before a large roar filled the room. Rita covered her ears before her eardrums popped. Rory shouted in pain and let Rita go as the force of Maverick's roar almost caused him to shift. Rita scrambled out of the way. She hurried to Maverick and threw herself in his arms whimpering against his chest. She knew that acting like she needed him was going to be a huge boost to his ego.

"Thank god you're here," She whispered knowing he could hear her. He rubbed her arms and held her protectively.

"Didn't I tell you they were off limits?!" he roared at Rory.

"You forgot you took a vow to me? That I'm your alpha? That I can feel you? You were so damn excited to fuck one of my girls that you didn't even block your feelings and they came straight to me. That's how I knew you were on some fuck shit. If you want a wolf, then I suggest you go out there and snatch one up for yourself. Touch another one of my girls, and I'll pump you full of wolfsbane." With that said, Maverick held Rita at the waist and led her away from the room. Even though she was pretending to need Maverick she was thankful that he did come in time to save her. She was going to be in Jayce's arms again, and the last thing she wanted to have to admit was that she had to suck the dick of another wolf. But if she had to do it to protect Maya, Brandy, and Amber, she would do it again.

Maverick carried her back to his large bedroom. Hera sat up in bed smiling, but that disappeared the moment she saw that Rita was with him.

"Get out and leave us alone," Maverick ordered Hera.

"Excuse me?" Hera asked.

"Did I stutter or are you deaf?" Maverick gritted. Hera slowly climbed out of the bed.

"Where is it that you expect me to go?"

"Do you see how big this damn house is? Find somewhere. As a matter of fact, I'm hungry. Be a good female and make me something to eat." Hera cut her eyes at Rita before she left the bedroom. Maverick turned and looked at Rita.

"Are you okay?" he asked her. Rita had to hide her surprise.

"Not really," she spoke softly. "I thought he was going to force me to fuck him."

"Well, you don't have to worry about any of that ever again."

"What about the girls? If he doesn't get me he'll just go back and try to get them."

"Don't worry about them either. No one will touch them except me when they are ready to be bred." Rita hugged herself and looked at him.

"Are you going to whip me anymore?" she asked.

"Are you going to disobey and disrespect me?"

"No. I learned my lesson," she said touching the scars on her stomach.

"Then I won't have to put my hands on you." Rita began to think about her chances of escaping without having to have sex with Maverick. It was slim to none. That was the only fault to her plan. But maybe there was nothing she could do about that.

"Are you going to be rough with me?" she asked him. He looked her up and down before licking his lips.

"Is that the way you like it?" he asked.

"No," she scoffed.

"Then I won't be rough." He looked towards the bed.

"Get on the bed." Rita slowly climbed onto the bed then turned to look at him. He spent some time texting wildly on his phone. After 20 minutes he looked back at her and the way she was positioned on the bed. Smiling, put down his phone and came over to her. He pushed her to lay down softly and opened her legs. She snapped her eyes shut as he bent over to lick her womanly folds. It was so hard forcing herself not to cringe at his tongue on her. When your mind was filled with your mate, there was nothing about another male that could appease you. And right now, Rita felt nothing but his wet tongue as he lapped at her insides.

"Hm, you taste good," he commented as he drew her lips into his mouth for a final slurp. He rose up and looked at her with his erection hard in his jeans. Rita could sense he wanted to do more than just taste her, but the door opened, and Hera walked back into the room. She froze and glared at them.

"What are you doing?" she asked.

"You took too long with my food. And I had to eat something," Maverick replied snatching the plate she had in her hand. He set the plate down at his desk then motioned for Rita to come to him. Rita slid off the bed and walked to him allowing him to make her sit on his lap. He began feeding her the eggs and home fries that Hera had made.

"That food was for you not for her!" Hera snapped.

"Hera you got one more time to open your fucking mouth and annoy me," he snapped back at her. She quickly shut her mouth and crossed her arms. When Maverick wasn't looking Rita smirked at Hera to get her even more upset, and it worked. Rita held onto Maverick and let him feed her. Once the food was done he picked her up and carried her to the bed.

"Get some rest. I have to go back out and do what I was going to do before the vibes Rory was sending through our link distracted me. I won't be back for a couple of hours."

"So she's staying in my bed?" Hera asked. Maverick ignored her.

"Make sure you don't cause any trouble today Hera. Leave Rita be, and I won't shove my foot up your ass. Make sure the rest of the girls are taken care of."

"Wait, can I come with you?" Rita asked him.

"Yeah right. I'm not falling for that one."

"My wolf needs to be let out Maverick. I'm going crazy. I figure it's safer to shift with you around than anyone else. Please? I'll do anything if you trust me with this." Maverick paced for a moment.

"Why should I trust you?" he asked.

"You have more power than me Maverick. You can hear my heartbeat and know there's no deception. My wolf wants to stretch herself out, and after earlier, I don't feel safe being here without you. And I've been wearing these silver cuffs for a couple of days. When they get taken off my wolf would still be too weak to do anything. I'll allow her to shift and then stretch then bring her back then you can put the cuffs back on." Maverick was quiet as he was indeed listening to her heartbeat. She was, in fact, speaking the truth.

Maverick figured this was a way to get a couple of things out of Rita. Either she would do something stupid, and he'd kill her. Or her wolf would do something instinctual that could perhaps lead him to where her pack had moved to. Or she'd be able to handle what he was about to do and become something more than his incubator for his pups. Maverick was still a little stuck on Bliss, but if he could get Rita to be completely allied with him and commit to a vow so he could be her true alpha then there was nothing Rita wouldn't do for him. And that included helping him capture Bliss.

"Let's go," Maverick said. He opened the door to the closet and tossed her a pair of jeans and a t-shirt.

"Hey, that's my clothes!" Hera shouted. Maverick quickly turned around with his hand up ready to backhand her. She quickly jumped out of the way to avoid his hit.

"Don't play with me," he gritted.

"You better just relax," Rita responded.

"Shut up! Think you're slick? All of a sudden you wanna act like you're on his side. I know you planning something shady and you're a fool Maverick if you think she's suddenly willingly to do what you want her to."

"Maybe that's because I tore her ass up enough for her to quit playing games," Maverick said.

"Looks like you're gonna need some of what she got since all of a sudden you got this big ass mouth that I keep warning you about." Hera crossed her arms and dropped down into a chair getting quiet. Rita quickly dressed in the clothes Maverick tossed her.

"Make sure you look after the girls," Maverick warned her before he and Rita left the room. She had to hide her excitement at finally being able to be let out of the house and to figure out where an exit was. Maverick went down a flight to the first level of the house before turning a corner and walking by the kitchen and then going down the long hallway. The large door that seemed would be the front door, he didn't even pay attention to.

"Front door?" Rita asked him pointing to it.

"Yes. But we don't use that door."

"Oh." She continued to follow him to the end of the hall away from the front door to the back door. She watched him closely as he punched in a number to a keypad that opened the door with a click.

2701, she thought to herself, saying it over and over so she wouldn't forget it. When he turned and looked at her, she averted her eyes to make it look like she wasn't watching him punch in the code. He stepped outside, and she followed him. A sigh of relief escaped her when the morning breeze brushed against her body. She took a moment to close her eyes and take in the feel of finally being outside.

"Feels good huh?" Maverick asked her.

"So good," she smiled. "Thank you for letting me come out with you."

"Just keep up." Maverick led the way through the backyard that expanded out into woods. Trees surrounded the whole house it seemed, and the rugged downhill terrain let Rita know that were must have been on a mountain. She tried to project to Kellan and Bliss, but her powers were diminished. And taking the cuffs off will release her wolf, but it would take some hours for her powers to get back to its full strength. So she wasn't lying when she told Maverick there would be no escaping for her. And even if she could Rita wasn't going to escape and leave the three girls behind. That could chance them getting hurt by Maverick's anger that she had run off.

Maverick led the way across the backyard and down towards the woods where the terrain got a little bit more rugged. Once they were deep in the woods, Maverick used his senses to make sure there was no one nearby before he continued walking. They hiked for what seemed like a half hour. Maverick wanted to walk further to tire her out before he took the cuffs off, but Maverick was mistaken. Hiking through the forest jumping over fallen trees, tree stumps and maneuvering through the rugged terrain did little to tire her out. She kept up with Maverick the entire time. When they reached the midpoint of where he was headed he stopped in a clearing.

"Alright undress," he ordered. Rita looked around the forest slightly and recognized nothing. She didn't want to make it obvious she was looking around, so she undressed quickly while still scanning. But still she'd never been in this part of the woods before.

When she was undressed, he approached with a key to the cuffs. Her heart began to beat faster at the anticipation that she could finally give her wolf a chance to break free. And the moment the cuffs were off her wrists the pressure of the suppression of her powers lifted and that alone made her weak. When the cuffs came off her ankles she fell to the ground as the rush of her power came over her too quickly for her weakened body to handle. Her breathing was strained as her wolf pushed forcefully through the invisible barrier. When it broke, she screamed as she gave into a painful shift. Her bones cracked and contorted before her wolf emerged from her body and stayed limply on the ground too weak to move. Even though her shift was painful she was in the most relief in her wolf form and feeling the power that she was born with as a shifter.

Maverick was looking at her closely, and Rita just knew he was waiting for her to do something. So she did absolutely nothing. She laid there and just enjoyed her time without the silver cuffs on. Seeing she wasn't going to do anything useful to him, he turned his back towards her and scanned the area. It was still quiet and clear, so Maverick decided to keep moving forward.

"Come on," he said turning to her. She got up slowly, and after stretching deeply, her wolf receded and allowed Rita to return to the surface. She redressed in her clothes. Thankfully Maverick didn't put the cuffs back on her, but she paid attention to what he did with the keys.

They continued their hike through the woods. Rita kept a wall up in her mind to make sure she wasn't accidentally projecting her thoughts to Maverick. She was too weak still to project to Bliss or Kellan. Even though she couldn't project to her alpha's, Maverick was close enough for her to accidentally project to him without her realizing it.

Alpha. Beta. Omega. Fuck Rita, I'm going nuts without you. I can't walk around saying Alpha, Beta, Omega all fucking day. I just want you back. Hearing Jayce's fierce voice in her mind made her stumble. She tripped over her feet, but Maverick kept her from falling by grabbing onto her elbow and keeping her up.

"You okay?" he asked.

"Yes, still weak," she replied with a smile. If Maverick had any clue, she could hear her mate that would be the end of any plan she had. But the fact that she could hear him made her realize he must have been close. Her wolf began yearning for their mate, but Rita comforted her to just give it some time. The moment Maverick let her go and kept walking, Rita sighed. She was trying to regulate her heartbeat. Any change would alert Maverick that something was up. And speaking with her mate could change her heartbeat for sure. But she wasn't going to let this chance slip by.

Jayce?

****

Jayce sat straight up in bed like a springboard. Rita's sophisticated voice filtered through his mind ever so slightly. Was he finally going crazy? Was he hearing things? He scooted down on his bed until his legs hung off the edge. After his punishment, he was in his room trying to mind speak to his mate because he had nothing else to do. The rest of the pack was planning on investigating Maverick's businesses to search for clues to finding Rita. He, of course, was left out because he couldn't control his damn self.

Jayce I know you hear me, Rita spoke again, firmer. *I just heard you talking to me. Unless you went batshit crazy and walking around here rogue and can't control your damn thoughts.* In such a situation like this, Jayce couldn't imagine himself even smiling, but the attitude of his mate always got to him. She was just so different.

Rita, baby? He asked. *Where are you?*

I don't know. We're walking through the woods. Jayce hopped off his bed and ran out of his room. He shot through the tunnels and skidded into the large kitchen where the rest of the pack were sitting around the table, eating.

"I can hear her," Jayce shouted. "Rita, she's speaking in my head." Kellan stood immediately.

Rita? Kellan spoke. If she was close enough to speak to Jayce, then she was close enough to speak to anyone else.

Kellan!

Project to me Rita. Show me where you are, Kellan urged.

I can't. Too weak.

"Fuck!" Kellan shouted. "Tristan let's go. Jaxson stay with the females."

"I'm coming with you!" Jayce said. Kellan looked at Jayce hard. The man was out of control but if it were Bliss, Kellan wouldn't want anyone else to save her but him.

"Fine. But you follow orders Jayce, and I mean it." Jayce just nodded and turned around running towards the exit.

I'm coming for you baby, Jayce said to Rita.

We're walking, I don't know where we're going.

Howl Rita, so I can find you, Kellan ordered.

I can't! I can't do anything but mind speak. Oh my god, we're going into another pack territory. I can smell the different wolves. I'm scared he's going to do something horrible.

Just hang in there baby, Jayce told her. Outside of their cave, Tristan, Jayce, and Kellan split up into three separate directions with their noses to the sky.

"I got her scent," Tristan shouted from his direction. Both Kellan and Jayce headed in his direction. All three of them caught her scent, but it was far off.

"Let's go," Kellan ordered. He led the charge in the direction of where Rita's scent was coming from.

Jayce! He's putting the- Rita's voice cut off in his head.

Rita? Rita!

"Kellan she can't mind speak anymore. She's gone!" Jayce shouted. Jayce ran faster, running past his pack mates to get to his mate before he lost her again.

Rita tried to protest against Maverick putting the cuffs back onto her wrists and ankles, but he wasn't having it. He cuffed her, and all ties to her mate zapped out. All her superior senses shrunk into their human uses. If Jayce was going to find her, he would have to do it without her help.

"Keep quiet," he ordered her as he dragged her through the brush and onto pack territory. All the wolves gathered around the pond stopped what they were doing and looked at Maverick immediately.

"Can we help you?" One of the wolves said, standing. He seemed to be the one in charge since he spoke first. Rita wondered why they hadn't sensed an intruder coming long before Maverick entered their territory unless this wasn't really their territory and they were just passing by.

"Who's alpha?" Maverick asked. The wolf who'd spoken first started walking towards Maverick.

"Who you think?" he asked pulsing his alpha vibes at them. Rita felt the power of his wolf, but thankfully it didn't affect her as much because her wolf was trapped by the silver. Without another word, Maverick unsheathed his claws and swung them at the wolf's neck. Rita screamed in terror as blood gushed from the alpha's wound. The alpha fell to the ground struggling to breathe. All at once, his pack mates were ready to attack. The submissive wolfs took off while the dominant ones were coming to fight. A she-wolf ran straight at Rita. She didn't even have to think about a mode of attack before the she-wolf was on her. Rita flipped the wolf over and immediately put her into an armbar. Maverick was busy fighting off the other wolfs and decimating them to pay attention to Rita.

"You have to run as far away as you can and warn the rest of your pack," Rita whispered to her. The she-wolf immediately still, listening to Rita.

"See the silver cuffs I have on? He's keeping my wolf trapped, and I can't escape. If you stick around you're going to end up like me. I'm going to pretend to break your arm, and you need to run off." The she-wolf nodded. Rita screamed and pretended to bend her arm past its capacity. The she-wolf screamed before she broke from Rita's grip and scrambled away running. Maverick grabbed up Rita and began dragging her away.

"Time to go," He growled. Instead of heading back the way they came he took her to the pond an threw her in before following suit himself. He was trying to get rid of their scents. He dragged her out of the water and immediately slung her over his shoulder as he ran through the woods.

"What are you doing?!" Rita shouted at him.

"I smell wolves coming!" Aside from that, he said nothing as he ran through the forest with her on his shoulder. As she hung, tears ran down her face. The wolves he probably smelled was the wolves that would come to her rescue. Maverick didn't stop running until he reached the terrain of the large house they were occupying. He dropped her to the ground.

"Why did you attack those wolves?" she asked.

"They go to that pond every day after a pack run. I figured it's easier to take out a pack who aren't on their territory. Without an alpha, those wolves will need someone to look after them. I told you before I want to be the reigning alpha. Every single alpha nearby will have to face me because I will take over."

"Oh," was all Rita could manage to say.

"And like I said. If I have you and Bliss at my side, they'd be no one who could challenge us. Kellan would probably die at losing his mate. I saw the way you handled that she-wolf. Even with the cuffs on you managed to have her running off."

"Well, she was coming after me, and I'm pretty sure she was going to come after you too, so I had to do something." Maverick looked her up and down.

"You surprise me, Rita. I had all intentions that you were going to escape, and I would have to kill you."

"I don't come from a good pack Maverick. I was an Omega before I went to Kameron's pack. And then I found my mate who didn't want the same things I wanted. I haven't been happy in Kellan's pack because Jayce and I were having problems. Maybe that mating shit isn't for me. Obviously, when you first attacked the pack, I couldn't help that my wolf kind of went rogue to protect Jayce in the first place. And then when I got here, all I could do was bad mouth you, cuss at you, and fight back because I was afraid. And I wanted to hide my fear, so I acted tough. Now I have these scars all over my damn body, and I feel so stupid for not just giving in. I don't wanna fight anymore. Hell, I haven't fit anywhere else in my life. Maybe this is somewhere I can fit. I'm tired of being powerless. Time to change that. I guess it helps that I saw you're pretty good in bed too."

"Last time I tried to get you Rita, you ran off to Kellan."

"Because I was tryna save face for my mate. We're not going to be together, so it doesn't make sense doing that anymore."

"You think you can prove that to me?" Maverick asked. Rita looked at him with a small smirk. She tried to appear seductive, but that was not one of her strong suits at all. Thankfully, he fell right into that trap.

"Come on," he said nodding his head towards the mansion. Rita sighed and smiled at him before following him back to the mansion.

Chapter Nine

"I smell blood!" Tristan shouted as he ran behind Kellan and Jayce. Both wolves turned their noses up and smelled the air. Jayce cursed loudly and began running harder.

"I can't smell her anymore," he breathed in a panicked tone. And he was right to be panicked. None of them could smell her. There was just the stickiness of coagulating blood in the air around them. They burst through a large line of brush into a clearing around a pond. Wolves were gathered around a fallen wolf who was bleeding out from his neck. A female stayed kneeling next to the wolf while the males turned to Kellan ready to attack. But they were all submissive wolfs. Kellan let his canines fill his mouth before growling at them, and then roaring. They bowed immediately at his alpha vibes.

"What happened?" he asked.

"Another alpha came by and attacked us," one of the wolves answered.

"Our alpha, he's dying." Kellan peered down at the alpha. He was indeed dying.

"Gather around him," Kellan ordered.

"Everyone put their hands on him." They did as Kellan asked.

"Feel his life force through the bond you have with him from the vows you made. Once you can feel his pulse, I want you to feed his pulse with healing energy." Power crackled through the air as the wolves fed their alpha with pack energy to heal. The alpha's eyes opened and glowed with the force of his wolf. He roared as healing energy was forced into his body allowing his wounds to start to stitch back together.

"Release him!" Kellan ordered. If they held on for too long the power would be too overbearing. Plus, they would deplete themselves of energy. The wolves let go and fell onto the ground breathing heavily. The alpha gave a final jerk before his eyes dimmed and closed. His wounds continued to stitch together showing that he had successfully fallen into a healing sleep.

"Did you recognize the man that attacked?" Kellan asked.

"No. he just came out of nowhere. Dell wasn't ready for the attack, and that's why he got bested," the she-wolf spoke. Kellan figured Dell was the alpha.

"I don't smell her," Jayce said confirming that Rita's scent was completely gone.

"Her?" the she-wolf asked. Jayce looked at her.

"There was a woman with the man that attacked us." Jayce immediately got in her face.

"What'd she look like? Did she say anything to you? Was she hurt?!" Jayce's control began to quiver. Kellan pulled him away from the she-wolf with a growl. Jayce's wolf bowed down in respect for its alpha.

"What's your name?" Kellan asked her.

"Mira," she replied.

"We happened to be looking for a wolf, and her scent led us this way, but then we lost it."

"Well, she was wearing silver cuffs," Mira informed him.

"She had dark brown skin, long sister locks, and a septum piercing." Jayce was growling behind Kellan as Mira described his mate to a tee. It was indeed Maverick who attacked the small pack.

"I attacked her," Mira confessed.

"You did what?!" Jayce shrieked. Kellan pushed him back to keep him from getting in her face again. Mira had very small dominant vibes so she could easily be spooked by a fully dominant wolf. She was however tall and elegant with long wavy curls as if she was from native and African descent mixed. Her almond skin tone was flush with fear.

"I thought she was going to attack us too," Mira explained.

"But then she put me in an armbar and told me to run. She said she was being held captive and if I didn't get out of there, he was going to capture me too. So she pretended to break my arm to make it look like she'd won the fight and I ran away afraid! But if she hadn't warned me so I could run off, he would have taken me with him too!" Jayce paused from pacing. His mate even captured had managed to help another wolf.

"The other wolves were trying hard to fight him off, but we're not as dominant. Thankfully something spooked him, and he took the she-wolf swam across the pond and ran out on the other side."

"Fuck!" Jayce screamed.

"We spooked him! He knew we were coming and took off with her! We can't smell her anymore because they went in the water!" Jayce was shaking in his anger. His eyes began to glow, and his wolf's mouth was dripping with saliva, foaming at the mouth ready to attack because he wanted someone to feel his pain at being close enough to getting his mate back and then having her slip right through his fingers.

"Jayce," Kellan growled. "Pull your animal back," he ordered. Jayce tried to fight his wolf from emerging. His breathing became labored and hoarse as his muscles began to pop and shift. His canines came out next.

"Get away from me," Jayce gritted unable to pull his animal back. He doubled over as he fought the shift. Kellan stood in front of him.

"I'm not going anywhere. As both your alpha and your friend," Kellan said. A breeze passed between them carrying Kellan's uniquely mixed scent to Jayce's senses. In that scent, he was reminded of Bliss. What she had taught him came to the forefront of his mind. He closed his eyes immediately.

"Alpha. Beta. Omega," he growled out visualizing what he loved most about his mate. Her scent, her attitude, her beauty. He surrounded himself with her aura while repeating the mantra. His wolf whined and howled in sadness but began to retreat. He eventually flopped down with tears leaking from his eyes at the memory of his mate. Jayce fell to his knees with those same tears streaking down his face.

"You did it. You controlled him," Kellan said. Jayce sniffled.

"Bliss taught me how. Taught me to wrap myself in everything I love about my mate and say the damn mantra. It works to control him, but it doesn't unbreak my heart to the fact that she's still gone. That she's still being held against her will." He wiped the tears from his face.

"But I'll find my girl. No matter what it costs me."

"I'm so sorry," Mira spoke up. She walked up to Jayce and put her hand on his shoulder. A strange feeling came over him. It wasn't so strange the type of feeling it was it was strange in the fact that it wasn't his feelings. But yet still a sense of relief, comfort, and warmth filled him. Jayce knocked her hand off him.

"The hell are you doing?" he asked.

"I'm an empath," she replied.

"I can feel emotions and draw them into myself, so the person can get a sense of relief." Jayce looked her up and down. He knew there were plenty mystical beings on this planet, but he'd never met any of them.

"So if you take my sorrow away you have to deal with it?" Jayce got his answer when he saw a tear roll down her face. She wiped it away quickly.

"It doesn't last that long, but it takes its toll sometimes."

"I've never heard of a shifter empath," Kellan spoke up.

"Well, my mother was the empath. She was in a native American tribe when she met my father who was a shifter. Everyone thought I would have one of the gifts. I've been an empath since I was born. But when I was 18, I shifted under a full moon with the rest of the pack. So, here I am."

"Interesting," Jayce said. He stood and looked at Kellan.

"What now?"

"We need to go back to our territory and figure some things out."

"We can carry Dell back to-" Kellan cut Mira off.

"All of you come with us. The rest of you need to heal and wait for your alpha to come out of his healing sleep. Once he does, you can continue onto your own territory."

"Thank you alpha," Mira sighed.

"Kellan," he smiled at her. "Let's go." He and Tristan lifted Dell to carry him to their large cave while the others followed them. Mira smartly walked next to Jayce soaking up his emotions for him and allowing him to stay calm for the journey back.

Bliss was waiting for them at the entrance of the cave. The moment they climbed through the waterfall there she was waiting to greet them. Kellan put Dell on the ground and kissed his mate. He introduced her as the alpha female before letting them into the cave.

"It looks like Maverick is attacking any pack he finds," Kellan said.

"This time he attacked this pack with Rita at his side. He was able to get away before we found them."

"So what do we do now?" Bliss asked.

"We have the locations of all his businesses. And tonight we make the move to search each and every one. I don't plan on stopping the search until we have Rita or something concrete. Even if it takes us all night," Kellan replied.

"So we should all rest up and prepare," Bliss said.

"You, Kyra, and Gemma are not coming with us," Kellan said sternly before walking off. He led the other pack to the living area where they could relax before helping to carry Dell to a vacant room to sleep off the rest of his healing. Even if he'd walked away from Bliss she was talking angrily in his head cursing him about his choice to exclude her. When he went back to the kitchen where he'd left her, she was still there standing with her arms crossed.

"You don't have the power to tell me what to do you know," she said. Kellan groaned in frustration.

"Bliss," he growled.

"Leave me alone before I end up saying something rude. I'm your fucking alpha. I gave an order. That's it. Ask anyone what the punishment is for disobeying an order." He grabbed a bottle of beer before stomping away. Bliss rolled her eyes and looked at the she-wolves.

"I don't understand why I'm the alpha female if I don't get a say in what goes on," Bliss shook her head.

"You are the alpha female Bliss, but Kellan is still the alpha too. And if you would have given an order I'm pretty sure he would follow you," Kyra said.

"Maybe you should be open to compromise a little bit more instead of being quick to pull the alpha card. No one is challenging your role. And you, out of us all should listen to Kellan the most. He is your mate after all," Gemma added. Bliss sighed and crossed her arms. For a moment she dropped her feelings and focused on her mate. Sure enough he was agitated, and hurt. Bliss suddenly felt like the bitch she'd been treating her mate like.

"Oh no," she sighed. She ran off without another word to the direction of Kellan. She found him in their bedroom pacing. He was drinking his beer while digging his claws into his palm on his free hand.

"What are you doing?" Bliss asked. She went over to him and unclenched his hand. He began to heal immediately.

"I'm frustrated, and self-pain helps me not inflict pain on anyone else."

"I'm sorry," Bliss blurted out.

"You're right. You are the alpha, and even though I wanna be fighting at your side, I have to be smart about my role here. And I feel like such a bitch for causing you all this damn trouble. When I should be sticking by your side. If you don't wanna be mated anymore, then I understand how you-"

"Bliss," he waved her off.

"Wolves don't break up," he said. "Not after completing the mating bond. We will always have our differences, but I'm here to protect and love you. And I need you by my side. No king was ever successful without a queen. I'm nothing without you, and our bond makes us more powerful than any other being out there. That's why we have to stay on the same page. Maverick is collecting women. I can't willingly bring women out there to fight him. It wouldn't make sense. So I need you to understand that when I make orders, I don't do it for my own good. Being dominant is a double edge sword Bliss. It's hard for me to submit. But if there was any wolf in this world that I would submit to, it'll be my mate. So if you can't submit to me Bliss and know that I won't take advantage of you, then we're going to be in for a rocky relationship."

"I don't want to make it hard on us," she said.

"And I'll try. I promise I will." She went down on her knees as a sign of submission. Kellan leaned over and kissed her on the forehead.

"Don't make me have to give you this talk again," he warned. "Because we won't be talking." He got down on his knees in front of her as well and embraced her in a hug before kissing her deeply.

****

Rita appeared calm as Maverick paced around the kitchen, slamming things and punching the walls. Amber, Maya, and Brandy were sitting around the table eating quietly. Rory and Levi were posted up against the walls. Maverick was pissed off about a couple of things. His plans weren't going as he imagined. Including Hera still not in heat.

"I can't believe you're still not in heat," Maverick grunted.

"They said the medicine would work."

"It's human medicine. It shouldn't work on us," Rita said. Maverick looked at her. After what happened earlier he was still trying to figure something out with Rita.

"I smelled him in the woods. Kellan," he said.

"That's why I ran away through the water. But I wanna know how he found us."

"She was probably trying to trap you," Hera snorted.

"You know that's not true," Rita spoke up for herself.

"So is the pack close to here?" Maverick asked her.

"I don't know where here is Maverick!" she exclaimed. "And truthfully I didn't tell you where my pack was because I didn't know where they went."

"She's full of it," Hera snapped.

"Shut up," Maverick gritted. He looked at Rita.

"You're going to help me capture your old pack," he ordered. He was expecting a doubtful or a scared reaction, but Rita simply shrugged.

"Okay," she said. "But if I go up against Kellan you have to protect me no matter what. If I have your protection, then we have a deal. And I want to be your alpha female," Rita added looking at Hera. Maverick simply smiled.

"If you can prove to be a promising alpha female then the gig is all yours."

"You can stay here, or you can come and find out," Rita smiled turning and walking away.

"Don't fall for her trap!" Hera screeched. Rita made sure to wink at the girls as she left the kitchen, so they understood she didn't mean any of what she just said. But for her outcry, Maverick slapped Hera hard sending her to the ground. She fell in a heap before Maverick followed after Rita. So far she was looking like one of the best choices he made. The other three wolves were quiet and seemed content with the fact that this was where they were going to live now. The only person ruining things was Hera. And Maverick was getting real sick of her.

"She's going to ruin things," Rita said as they entered his large bedroom. "Hera."

"Don't worry about her," Maverick grunted.

"I'll fix her up just like I fixed you up." Rita slid onto the bed nerves beginning to take over. Was she really about to give herself to a wolf that wasn't her mate? It seemed so wrong, but she knew it was the only way to eventually rescue herself and the three wolves. And if she had to sacrifice herself then so be it.

"I'm not really good at this," she said pulling down her pants slowly. Maverick watched her as she stripped.

"So you're going to have to tell me how you like it." Rita knew that feeding into his ego would gain her more points, so she was going for it.

"First I'm going to taste you again," he said. "And then I want you on top of me. Showing me, you can be the alpha female." Rita nodded and fell back onto the bed with her legs splayed open. Like the first time; when his tongue touched her insides, all she felt was the wetness of his mouth slobbering over her. There was no pleasure, and she had to force herself not to be disgusted. But he was moaning and groaning like his life depended on it, and she knew she had to show some sort of excitement. Closing her eyes, she envisioned Jayce's face. She didn't think about Jayce being the one licking her right now. She made sure to just conjure up the memory of when he did have his tongue on her. And that's what made her moan. That's what powered her to show any kind of emotion to Maverick.

"Oh Maverick," she moaned. "It feels so good." But it didn't. Thinking of Jayce just allowed for her moans to be real.

"That's how a real wolf does it," he said. Rita rolled her eyes but continued to moan. He rose up after giving her one last lick. He stood and began undoing his pants. Thankfully his dick wasn't ugly. Then she would have a hard time pretending to like.

"Before I have you on top I just want a little sample," he groaned. Pushing her legs back he nudged her opening with his tip. Again, Rita was thanking the heavens that Maverick's size didn't compare to Jayce's whatsoever. She snapped her eyes shut still as he penetrated her body. His moans of pleasure made her cringe. She didn't want anyone feeling pleasure from her body but Jayce, but there was nothing for her to do now.

"I can't wait until you're in heat," he growled as he began to move faster and faster. "If you feel this good now you're gonna be fucking amazing in heat." Rita grabbed hold of his shoulders as he began thrusting harder and she had nothing else to hold onto. And the moment she did hold onto him he began fucking her ferally as if he couldn't get enough. He clasped his hand around her throat and pummeled her into the mattress. She felt him swelling inside her and was thinking hard about not getting his seed inside her. Even if she was giving herself to him, making him spill his seed inside her was another level that she refused to climb. Seeing no other option, she pushed at him until he rolled over and got herself on top of him.

"I thought you wanted me to ride it," she growled sexily. He dug his claws into her hips with a creepy smile on his face. She grinded against him which she wasn't necessarily good at but because his dick was smaller than Jayce's she was able to fake the funk. Maverick was in over his head with pleasure moaning and groaning as if this was the first time he ever had sex. Leaning forward, she braced her hands against his chest and rode him harder. His dick swelled inside her, and he let out a groan from deep within his gut. Rita quickly moved off of his dick letting it flop outside of her just as he released his seed. She wrapped her hand around his softening shaft and jerked him off so he couldn't complain about her not letting him come inside her. Breathing heavily, Rita sat on his lap and watched him catch his breath. An enormous amount of guilt began to filter through her body. She knew why she did what she did, but that didn't ease up the guilt. She felt embarrassed and used.

"Damn Rita," he groaned slapping her ass.

"You're just a good a piece of ass like Bliss was. I see threesome's in our future." He rose up on his elbows.

"Think you can keep up?" Rita teased him, trying to push her guilt away, so he didn't sense it.

"Keep up?" he smiled. He carefully picked her up and moved her to the side so he could get up. He went into the bathroom for a warm wash cloth that he brought back to Rita. She couldn't clean herself fast enough. He wiped himself down, but already Rita saw him getting aroused.

"Come here," he said lowly taking her by the ankle. Rita allowed him to pick her up, wrapping her legs around his waist. He placed her against the far wall next to the large window still holding her up. He found her entrance again and forced his way inside her. Rita wrapped her arms around his shoulders and buried her face in his neck, so she didn't have to look at him. With her legs wrapped tightly around his waist, he began grinding within her. Naturally, her body's response to penetration provided lubrication for his thrusts. He thought it was because she enjoyed it, but really it was just mother nature.

"You're gonna be my alpha female," he grunted. Rita sensed the change in his voice. She picked her head up from his neck to see his canines had filled his mouth. Before she could squirm out of reach, he was biting down on her neck. Rita's system was shocked by the bite. Her wolf inside her stood at attention growling at the unfamiliar bite. She was ready to charge at the intruder, but the silver cuffs kept her from emerging. But he was doing it whether she wanted him to or not. He was marking her.

The door to the bedroom burst open. Hera stood in the doorway holding one of the guns they use to shoot wolfs bane at wolves.

"Maverick!" Rita yelled. But he was too stuck on biting her. Hera aimed the gun at his back and shot twice. Maverick's teeth pried from her skin, ripping her flesh. She let out a scream of agony as purple smoke rose from Maverick's wounds. He slipped out of her and fell to the ground.

"I'm supposed to be the alpha female! I'll kill you and ruin all your plans before I let you throw me to the side like trash. Matter of fact I think I'll take over from where you left once you and your cronies are all fucking dead!" She aimed the gun towards Rita and squeezed the trigger, but nothing shot out.

"Fuck!" she screamed. Hera dropped the gun and ran out of the room. Maverick coughed on the ground trying to roll over. Again, Rita had to think on her toes.

"That bitch!" Rita screamed. "I'm gonna kill her!" She looked down at Maverick. "No one threatens our empire," she said.

"Go get that bitch," he coughed. Rita smiled evilly not because she wanted to attack Hera for Maverick, but because her plan was still working. Maverick was starting to get up and even though he was poisoned he would be able to burn it out of himself quickly. Rita moved fast, making sure to grab the key to the silver cuffs from the pocket of his jeans that were thrown on the floor. She bolted out of the room not even caring where Hera went. Running down the hall, she started to fear that Hera did something to the girls. She ran all the way back to the bedroom where they were being kept. Flying the door open she was happy to see they were unharmed.

"Thank goodness!" Rita breathed. They launched off the bed and gave Rita a group hug.

"Hera went nuts! She shot Rory and Levi with the wolfs bane and then ran to come and get you. Rory and Levi ran off somewhere with the poison in their bodies, and we just ran back to the room," Brandy said. Rita could tell in their inexperience that they didn't know what to do. But she was glad they hadn't taken off.

"Look, there's not much time," Rita said. She whipped out the key to the cuffs and immediately took them off. Each of the girls fell as the power of their wolves were released. Rita kept her composure as she got the cuffs off her wrists and her ankles.

"I know you're weak, but you have to fight through it. Let's go." Rita led the way out of the room and to the same door that Maverick had taken her through earlier. She hadn't seen Rory or Levi, so there was no one to stop them. As they ran past the kitchen, Rita grabbed a knife.

"We gotta go straight to the woods," Rita said.

"About a half hour of a walk is where I heard my mate. I think my pack is around there somewhere. It's just to find them." She punched in the code to the door that she remembered from earlier. As the door opened, Maverick let out a loud howl.

"Shit!" Rita cursed. "He's burning the wolfs bane out. We gotta-" A burning sensation ripped through Rita as the girls screamed. Turning around, Hera had the gun again, and this time it was reloaded with the poison.

"Run," Rita gasped as she fell to the ground, looking at the girls. With the knife in her hand, she cut the ends of one of her locks. She put it in Brandy's hand.

"GO!" The three wolves took off immediately, running at speeds to let Rita know that their powers were returning to their bodies. Rita knew she could beat Hera in a fight but with poison in her system, there was no way she would have enough strength. Hera strutted towards Rita, her canines dripping with saliva and her eyes the color of her wolf.

"You'll regret ever fucking with me little wolf," she spat. Maverick howled again, and this time it was with tenacity. The both of them felt his power throughout the house. Hera smiled evilly and turned the gun on herself and pulled the trigger. She grazed her shoulder with the wolfs bane. It wasn't enough to impact her completely, but it was enough to inflict pain. She growled and dropped the gun before jumping over Rita and sprinting out of the door.

Maverick thundered through the house running hard until he found Rita on the ground in front of the back door. Purple smoke was filtering through her stomach.

"Hera shot me," she gasped out.

"She let the girls go free and took the cuffs off me just to make sure my wolf felt the wolfsbane," Maverick growled in anger and scooped Rita up off the floor. He shut the door with his foot and carried Rita to the kitchen where he took a lighter and burned the wolfs bane out of Rita's body. She screamed as it left her body before she flopped down.

"Rory and Levi both got shot too," Rita said.

"I know. I feel it through our bond. I'll go burn out the poison with them in a minute."

"What are we going to do?" Rita asked.

"Hera is threatening everything," Maverick grunted and hit the counter with his fist.

"I don't know, but that shit pisses me off," he stated. "I need time to think." He scooped her up again and carried her all the way up to his large bedroom. He pulled out another set of cuffs and applied it to her wrist.

"Sorry baby girl. I gotta protect all my assets to a tee now." Rita tried not to cry as the power of her wolf was clamped down again. Maverick kissed her on the forehead before he left the room, closing the door. Rita threw her head back, slamming it against the bedhead. She sucked back her tears. Her plan had worked. She was able to get the girls free. But she was supposed to be with them. Now all she could do was wish the girls made it somewhere safe.

Chapter Ten

"Welcome back," Kellan greeted as Dell awoke from his healing sleep. He immediately pushed forth his alpha vibes, but Kellan showed no reaction. Dell was indeed an alpha, but his dominance was no match for Kellan. Kellan simply waved his vibes at the man and Dell was placated. He stood from the bed alert.

"You're an alpha," he said.

"Yes. I brought you and your pack here to my territory to heal up. The wolf that attacked you is a wolf that attacked my pack as well. We're making plans of attack."

"Let me and my pack help you," Dell offered.

"That wolf was confident in his attack. Means he studied my pack before he attacked."

"He's been attacking packs and trying to take their females," Kellan said. "He captured one of our she-wolves in fact." Dell looked around the room.

"Mira, where is she?" he asked worriedly. Kellan nodded towards the door then turned and walked out of the room, leading Dell to the kitchen where both their packs were having dinner.

"You're awake!" Mira burst out. She got up from the table to hug her alpha tightly. The rest of his pack gathered around him and hugged him as well. Kellan noticed that Mira was the only female in the pack.

"Is there others in your pack?" Kellan asked. Dell shook his head.

"It's only us. We were part of a larger pack, but they were mostly elders. Our last elder passed not too long ago leaving just us." Kellan nodded feeling sorry for the wolf. That's why being an alpha was more than just implementing rules. Being alpha meant that you were responsible for keeping your pack thriving and alive. No matter how many pack members Kellan did have he knew he and Bliss had to have pups. Having pups first not only ensured his bloodline of alphas but allowed for his pack to continue to grow. Kellan didn't know if Dell realized, but he needed to increase his pack numbers, or he would be in constant defense of other wolves who might deem him weak.

"Meet my pack," Kellan said. Everyone stood and introduced themselves. Jaxson came into the dining area out of breath. He'd been doing research the whole time in preparation for them to launch their attack.

"This is one of my enforcers, Jaxson." Jaxson shook the hand of the other alpha. Then he turned to Kellan and gave him the rundown of all he found. Jaxson looked at Mira and smiled. He knew the presence of other wolves were inside the cave, but he hadn't met any of them. Now seeing Mira, he was captivated by her beauty. But the way she was standing next to the alpha proved that she was off limits.

"Dell is going to come with us," Kellan said.

"He and his pack want to help."

"Good. Great to have allies. I think we should get moving as soon as the sun sets which is in an hour."

"Let's get ready then. Everyone to the meeting room so we can set the plans."

After a half hour of talking about modes of attack, the Phoenix Pack was ready. Jayce was on edge which was completely normal. But Kellan needed to be sure his beta wasn't going to lose control in any fight.

"I know you want to find Rita as much as we do," Kellan said.

"But you have to know that we can't afford you losing control."

"I know," Jayce replied. "I can't guarantee anything though. But if I start losing control knock me out. Do what you have to do." Kellan nodded.

"Who will stay here with the she-wolves?" Jaxson asked. "I want in on this one."

"No one has to stay and watch us," Kyra spoke up.

"We have a badass alpha female. She'll look out for us." Kellan looked at his mate who was nodding in agreement. He wanted her to trust him in anything he did which included letting him leave her behind. So in return, he had to trust her that she could protect herself and their pack if need be.

"I agree with Kyra," Kellan said. "The females can hold down the fort here. And I doubt that anything or anyone can even get in."

"Mira you can stay with the females," Dell said.

"I don't want to risk you out there in any fight." Mira just gave a nod instead of answering.

When the wolves were ready to leave; the pack traded hugs. Who knew what would happen out there. Kellan hugged Bliss for a long time unable to even let her go.

"Please be safe," she begged. Kellan kissed her deeply. Tristan saw his alpha kissing his mate and couldn't forget how Gemma's lips tasted. He hadn't tried to kiss her again. But if he was going out for a fight, he knew he should at least acknowledge her.

"If anything goes wrong Gemma, make sure to tear shit up," Tristan told her. Even if she was young and cute his mate was feisty.

"If I go down, it'll be with a fight," she said. Tristan smiled at her. Gemma looked as if she wanted to kiss him again, and he knew he should have just kissed her lips and settled her nerves, but he didn't. He kissed her forehead like she was some child and left it at that. And when he walked away, he felt like a complete idiot.

"Hey you," Kyra said to Jaxson. He looked at her.

"What's up?" He asked already smiling goofily.

"Just don't die bozo," she grinned. Jaxson plucked her nose before kissing her on the cheek. Even though he was close with all the she-wolves and respected them, he and Kyra connected on another level when they realized they were the only ones in the pack without mates. It allowed for them to have someone to be around when everyone else were busy worrying about their mates.

"Let's move," Kellan called out ready to go. The females followed them through the tunnels all the way to the opening of the cave. The waterfall was roaring in front of them keeping their scents masked from anyone who may come wandering. Dell seemed impressed by the cave itself seen as he didn't see it on his way in.

Leaving the cave, the Phoenix pack moved as a unit with Kellan in front, and Jayce to his right and Jaxson and Tristan walking behind them. They moved in this way for almost all their lives and now that they were officially in their own pack and had to protect it, things were much more real. Their plan was to head into town straight to Maverick's businesses, but they decided to follow the same direction of where Dell's pack was attacked. Since they were going into town, they hadn't decided to shift since they wanted appear as normal humans. But they were all healthy wolves capable of moving quickly without tiring easily.

"Wait," Jayce urged stopping immediately. They'd come by the clearing where Maverick had escaped after attacking Dell and his pack. Everyone halted and looked at Jayce. His amber wolf eyes shone back at them as his nose turned up to the sky. Kellan did the same thing.

"I smell her," Jayce said. "But her scent is different. Something's off."

"This way," Kellan pointing noticing Rita's scent as well. He led the way through the bushes towards the scent. The closer they got to Rita's scent was the more a mixture of scents began to hit them. Bursting out of the bushes they came upon three young female wolves who were trying to catch their breaths. They screamed in fright before whipping out their claws and standing defensively. One of them looked at Jayce.

"Jayce?" she asked.

"How the hell you know my name?" he questioned. The three wolves breathed a sigh of relief. They ran to Jayce, hugging him tightly and sobbing. Everyone just stared at them not sure what was going on.

"You must think we're crazy," one of the girls said. They backed off and dragged the other girls off Jayce.

"I'm Brandy," she said. "And this is Maya and Amber."

"And you know me how?" Jayce asked.

"Rita told us all about you. Told us that we might be able to find you out here if we kept moving. She gave us a piece of her hair. I think so if her pack was around they could scent her." Brandy showed him the lock that Rita had cut off.

"Maverick was holding you captive?" Kellan asked. The three girls looked at him and immediately lowered their heads to show him respect as an alpha. He could sense how submissive they were and also how young. They probably only just hit puberty.

"Yes. He attacked our pack and took us with him. Rita managed to get us out, but she's still stuck back at the house."

"House?" Kellan asked.

"That's where he's been keeping you?" The three of them nodded.

"Where is it?" They looked behind them and all around, but Kellan could tell they couldn't retrace their steps.

"We don't know," Brandy sighed.

"It's fine," Kellan told them. He turned and looked back at his pack. Jayce was mesmerized by the three wolves because they knew him because Rita told them about him, and the fact that she had helped them to get free despite her own captivity.

"What's the plan now?" Tristan asked.

"We've got to get them to safety. And figure out what house they're talking about," Kellan said.

"Then we're back out. Maverick might try to move Rita because they were able to escape. So we need to move fast."

"They're too weak to keep up," Jaxson noted. He went up to them and touched their wrists.

"They've been wearing silver cuffs. If it was taken off not too long ago, their strength is far from recovery. Even if they shift, the wolf would be weak."

"Easy fix. We carry them," Kellan said.

"Come on girls." Jaxson, Jayce, and Kellan each took one of the girls onto their backs. They were all thin and weighed very little.

"Wait, someone else is coming," Tristan said. They all got in defensive stances keeping the girls on their backs. Tristan and Dell stood in front of them since they weren't carrying one of the young wolves. But instead of something dangerous coming towards them, who emerged was another wounded she-wolf.

"Hera?!" Kellan gasped. She fell to the ground with purple smoke emanating from a wound on her shoulder.

"He shot me, but I got away," Hera breathed.

"Don't trust her," Brandy whispered in Kellan's ear. Going from the weary feelings rolling off his pack, Kellan knew they didn't trust Hera either. All Kellan knew was the woman always had something against his mother and father.

"You wanted to go with him," Jayce accused.

"You chose him despite what he was doing to the pack. Aren't you his so-called alpha female?"

"Not anymore," she said.

"He chose another alpha female and kicked me to the curb." The way she looked at Jayce sent a jolt through Jayce. She couldn't possibly mean that Maverick had taken Rita as his alpha female. No way.

"Kellan we need to move the fuck on," Jayce snapped. "I need my mate back."

"I can take you to him," Hera offered. "Right now!"

"It'll be a trap," Amber spoke in Kellan's mind. Kellan observed Hera. Unlike the young wolves, aside from the obvious wolfsbane wound, she didn't seem weak at all. There were no bruises from wearing silver, so truthfully being with Maverick was her choice. And he wasn't going to bring her back to their home where his mate and the rest of the she-wolves were.

"Tristan, you and Dell, and his wolves stay here with Hera. Make a fire and burn out the wolfsbane. Me, Jaxson and Jayce will bring the girls to safety." No one objected. Kellan turned and began running back towards their home. They moved so swiftly it was like they were gliding through the forest. The young wolves on their backs did little to slow them down. They reached the cave in no time.

Baby come to the front of the cave, Kellan spoke to Bliss through her mind. By the time they went under the waterfall, Bliss and the other she-wolves were waiting by the large door to enter the tunnels.

"Oh my god, I thought someone was hurt," Bliss sighed in relief. The young wolves jumped off their backs and huddled together as if they were shy. Gemma was probably the only one close to them in age. She was the one who stepped up to greet the young wolves to ease their nervousness.

"Hi, I'm Gemma," she greeted. The young wolves looked at her. They eyed her hard as if trying to recognize her.

"You look like two of our elders," Amber spoke up.

"Gina and Gabe. They came to our pack not long ago."

"Those are my parents," Gemma said.

"They told me the pack was attacked."

"Maverick captured Amber, Brandy, and Maya just like he captured Rita. They managed to escape with Rita's help, but she's still back there. We brought them here to be safe while we go back and get Rita."

"Go back where?" Gemma asked.

"This big house," Amber replied. Bliss gasped out loud and slapped her forehead.

"Oh my god! How could I have been so fucking stupid! His mansion Kellan! He's probably living there still!"

"Fuck," Kellan grunted. He looked at the young wolves.

"These are the females of my pack," he said.

"And Bliss is my mate. They will all keep you safe until the rest of us get back. You have nothing to fear now."

"She's counting on you to save her," Brandy said to Jayce.

"Please get to her before he does anything crazier." Jayce nodded. He was indeed going to get his girl. Kellan kissed Bliss one last time before they were leaving the cave and hurrying back to where they left the others.

Chapter Eleven

"We need to get out of here," Levi snapped at Maverick. He and Rory were recovering from the poison and appeared very shaken up.

"Calm down," Maverick said waving him off. They were back in the kitchen where Maverick was making Rita sit in his lap and still with the silver cuffs on.

"We're not safe here anymore. Hera, plus the other wolves got loose. Our location will be compromised." Maverick was worried about Rita's pack being out there in the first place. If he didn't know they were so close, he wouldn't care at all about their location being compromised. Hera had no one, and those three wolves didn't have the experience or the strength to retrace their steps and bring anyone here. But if Kellan and his pack were close like they were earlier anything was possible.

"They won't be able to find us," Maverick said.

"I wonder if this was the place you lived with Bliss," Rita spoke up.

"Because if they are out there like you scented them earlier they could be closing in on here because Bliss would be telling them about this place." Maverick slapped his forehead. He stood abruptly sending Rita flying out of his lap.

"This isn't the house I lived in with Bliss, but it's close enough. Shit." He began pacing. If they got close enough, there would be no trouble catching his scent or Rita's.

"So what are we going to do?" Levi asked.

"After the way we attacked them and kidnapped one of their she-wolves who just happens to be the Beta's mate they ain't going to come here looking to talk."

"What we need is time," Maverick said.

"And we don't have that right now."

"So why aren't we hightailing it out of here right now?" Rory asked.

"Fine, let's-" An emphatic howl ripped through the silence of the night time. Maverick was frozen. That wasn't just any howling wolf. It was the howl of an alpha.

"Kellan," Maverick gritted.

"How the hell are we gonna get out of this now?" Rory gasped.

"Shut up and stop being a bitch."

"Oh hell," Levi sighed as he sniffed the air.

"It ain't just Kellan. It's a whole bunch of them. And it's only three of us, and a weakened she-wolf. What the hell do you expect us to do?"

"Well we have wolfs bane, they don't," Maverick said.

"That's how we beat them the first time. So get the guns and let's go." He came towards Rita and grabbed her by the arm leading her towards the room where he kept his weapons. He grabbed hold of one of the guns before dragging her out of the room and towards the back door.

"What's the plan?" Rita asked.

"Fight out way out."

"You surely don't expect me to fight with these cuffs on do you?"

"I don't want you to fight at all." With Rory and Levi next to him, Maverick nodded towards the door. With guns in hand, Rory and Levi burst through the back door. Rita only got a glimpse of Kellan before Maverick shut the door keeping them inside.

Kellan knew he was going to be up against wolfs bane when dealing with Maverick from now on, but this time he was prepared. The moment Levi and Rory came charging out of the back door two of Dell's wolves attacked promptly. They had shifted while Kellan and his pack kept themselves in human form. Because Levi and Rory was so fixated on attacking Kellan, they weren't prepared for the attack that befell them. Kellan jumped into action when their guns fell to the ground. He grabbed the weapons and pointed them at Rory and Levi as they were being held down by the wolves from Dell's pack.

"I should pump both your asses full of this shit," Kellan gritted aiming the guns in their faces as they were being held down.

You do that, and your she-wolf dies, Maverick spoke into his head. Kellan jerked his head up and looked for the bastard. Sniffing the air, he could smell both Rita and Maverick inside the house on this side of the mansion. That was exactly why they had surrounded the back door in the first place.

Back away from the door, Maverick ordered. *Failure to do so and she's a goner. Don't fuck with me Kellan. Let my wolves up. I will tell them not to attack.* Kellan didn't want to listen to anything Maverick had to say, but he had to suck up his pride for Rita's life.

"Let them go," Kellan ordered.

"What?" Jayce screeched. "I don-"

"LET THEM GO," Kellan roared to the wolves. Even if he wasn't their alpha, his dominant vibes easily won them over. They let go of Rory and Levi, snarling as they backed away. Kellan also backed up from the front door to stand next to Jayce who was seething with anger.

"It's for Rita," Kellan said firmly. Jayce's eyes flashed between human and wolf as he tried to control his breathing.

"I'm about to lose my shit Kellan. And I swear to god I'm gonna start killing every fucking body left and right if I *don't get my mate right the fuck now,*" the last bit of his sentence was blurred between a growl and his normal voice. When Kellan looked at him, his features were beginning change his brows thickening and growing and his nose transforming into a snout. Even though they weren't werewolves they often appeared that way in between shifts when the human side was trying to control the shift.

Can't control your wolf, can you? Maverick cackled in Kellan's head. Jayce at the same time roared as he tried not to shift. Jaxson and Tristan held him down as he began to thrash and fight.

You better keep him away from me! Or else I'm going to kill her!

What the fuck do you want huh? I want my damn wolf back.

Same thing I wanted too but you refused to give in didn't you? Remember that, bitch? Maverick growled.

You know damn well I can't control a rogue wolf. So you decide what the fuck you're doing before he gets loose and come after you. At that point I can't stop him from ripping you to pieces." Maverick went quiet as he pondered what Kellan had just said.

"What are you going to do?" Rita asked, her voice shaking. She was slowly losing confidence in anything Maverick was about to do. And with her pack right there to save her, Rita didn't want her sacrifices to be for nothing. She didn't want to die when her freedom was this close.

"He doesn't have Bliss or the other she-wolves with him," Maverick said.

"Why would he? He knows this would be dangerous!"

"Now you can prove your loyalty to me," Maverick breathed into her ear.

"I will let you go. But you have to lure the she-wolves to me."

"What?"

"You heard me. They trust you. I have a club in town. You need to convince them to follow you there *without* the male wolves. Got that?" Rita had no other choice but to nod.

"When and where?"

"In one week. The place is called Rogue. You don't bring those wolves Rita, and it's your life on the line. But first, you're my ticket out of here." A booming roar once again filled the nighttime. Powers or not, Rita knew the sound of her mate. A feeling of dread filled her. Something was wrong with him.

"Let's go," Maverick ordered. He dragged her away from the back door and took her to a side door. He dragged her out of the house and towards the woods away from where her pack was

Kellan could scent Maverick on the move. But Jayce was in an intense battle for control that was going over the edge. He threw Tristan and Jaxson off him in all his fury. Kellan was deeply concerned because he still hadn't shifted. It was one thing to lose control and shift into your wolf, but it was another thing to lose control and not shift. If he didn't give control over to his animal, he was going to severe the tie he had to his wolf.

"Jayce just shift!" Kellan boomed.

"I'm gonna kill someone," he spoke his voice not even his own. Kellan understood the struggle, knowing that if he gave over to the wolf the animal would do something unthinkable. Kellan was going to force Jayce to shift, but Rita's scent caught his attention.

"They're running that way," Dell pointed out. Kellan took a step forward but had to stop when Maverick's voice filled his head.

Don't even bother. I'm letting your wolf loose. But you're going to have to let me go. You come after me she's dead. You let me go, and she's all yours. What's it going to be?

Just let her go, Kellan gritted. Maverick didn't answer him. Kellan began pacing feeling uneasy. This whole night had gone to shit, and he had no idea what the hell to do.

"You're just going to let him get away?" Hera asked him.

"Shut up," Kellan snapped.

"Weak son of a bitch," Hera spat at him. She headed towards the direction of Maverick's scent. Kellan didn't even bother to stop her.

The she-wolf that wants you is coming your way. Just make sure to send my wolf my way. Kellan told Maverick. Again Maverick didn't answer, but Kellan could still smell him, so he knew Maverick was still around.

Maverick got a couple of yards away from his mansion to a section of the woods that he knew would be safe for him to escape without being followed. He scented Hera coming close and didn't make any move. She came running through the woods until she bumped into him and Rita.

"Please take me back Maverick," she rushed out. Maverick glared at her. His trust was severed when it came to Hera, but he didn't doubt she could be useful to him. He let go of Rita and quickly unlocked her cuffs.

"Come," he ordered to Hera. He clamped the silver cuffs on Hera as Rita fell to the ground as her power resurfaced too strongly.

"But this time you're wearing silver cuffs," he said.

"Let's get the fuck outta here. Remember the plan, Rita." And then he was gone. Rita's senses were being distorted as her power was being restored. She didn't have the energy or the wherewithal to focus on what Maverick was doing. The scent of her pack filled her nose. Standing on shaky feet, she wobbled from tree to tree. Jayce's wolf was in distress more than Rita had ever experienced from him.

Jayce, she called out in his mind. *Jayce snap out of it. I'm free.* Rita clamped her eyes shut to focus on realigning her powers. She was going to fight through her weakness.

Rita? Baby? Jayce's heart rate began to slow hearing his mate's voice in his head. His wolf began to retreat giving Jayce all the control to go and get their mate. Her voice sounded weak in his head, so he knew she needed him. When he finally let his anger retreat all he could smell was his mate's sparkling scent. It smacked him so hard in his face he couldn't speak for a moment. Then he felt the pull of the mating bond. The bond that thumped harder and harder the more he craved his mate, the more he longed to have her in his arms. His wolf features receded bringing back his human brows and nose. Not wasting any time, he scrambled in the direction of his mate's scent.

Rita could smell Jayce getting close to her. She smiled weakly knowing that she was indeed free for the time being, and she would be back home with her pack. Fighting through her drained energy, she used the trees to help her move through the woods. She kept it up until she was able to move the pace of a jog.

"Rita!" Jayce called out for her.

"Jayce!" Her jog turned into a run. But then she spotted him. "Jayce," she sighed letting the words tumble from her mouth. Despite her weakened state, she felt her legs begin to move. And then she was full on sprinting. He was running towards her, jumping over branches and debris. They reached each other in seconds. Jayce caught his mate in his arms and held her tightly. Maverick's scent lingered all over her, but Jayce didn't even care. How could he when his mate was finally back in his arms. Her body trembled, and she held onto him as if she couldn't believe she was free,

"It's okay baby," he kissed her temple.

"I'm never letting you go." Hot tears streamed down her face landing on his shoulder. Jayce lifted her and wrapped her legs around his waist so he could carry her back. His wolf was prancing around with his tongue lolling out of his mouth in his content. Rita relaxed in his hold and closed her eyes feeling the security she'd been longing for.

Chapter Twelve

Jayce carried Rita all the way back to their new home. She was drifting in and out of sleep, the feeling of being in her mate's arms too comfy to resist. The rest of the pack walked with them, but their pace was slow lulling Rita to sleep even more. They walked for some time before Jayce was patting the side of her thigh lightly.

"We're here," he whispered to her. Rita pried her eyes open as the sound of a waterfall filled her eardrums. She blinked and gasped.

"Wow. What is this place?"

"This is our new home." Rita wiggled out of his hold and stood on her own two feet. She watched as Kellan led the way down the rock side before disappearing behind the trickling waterfall. Jayce knew she was still weak so he promptly picked her back up so he could carry her. She didn't argue, snaking around his body until she was on his back with her arms wrapped around his neck and her legs around his waist. He moved stealthily across the rock and climbed down to the waterfall before jumping behind it. Once he was on the other side, he put her down. Rita was in shock at the cavern behind the waterfall that was expertly hidden. It didn't even look like anything was behind the damn thing. This was the perfect place for a well-protected home.

Kellan used his handprint to open the large metal door embedded into the rock. Rita just kept gasping. The place was amazing. They walked through the door and followed a path into a large kitchen and dining area.

"Rita!" Bliss shouted in glee. Rita turned to see her alpha female rushing towards her. Rita burst out in happy tears as she ran to hug her pack mate. Gemma and Kyra appeared next; joining in on the hug.

"Thank goodness you're safe," Bliss breathed.

"I've been so stupid. I should have realized sooner he would have been near the house. I just-"

"It's done for," Rita cut her off. "I'm here now that's what matters."

"We missed you," Gemma said.

"Hell yeah," Kyra added.

"We are never going to let you out of our sights."

"Oh don't be dramatic," Rita laughed. She looked around the large space. "Wait! Did you guys find three young wolves?" Rita asked turning around to look at the men.

"Yes, they're here," Bliss answered.

"They were so weak I advised them that a healing sleep would do them well. They'll be awake by the morning." Rita sighed in relief thankful that they were able to be found.

"Look at you learning about wolves and shit," Rita teased her. They giggled and continued to hug.

"Alright break it up," Jaxson said.

"I didn't get to hug on my girl cause wolfman over there wasn't letting her go once he found her." Jaxson broke them up and grabbed Rita into his arms, hugging her tightly.

"None of us got to hug on her," Tristan said pulling Rita from Jaxson's hold and hugging her.

"But I should have had first dibs," Kellan said jerking her away from Tristan. "I am her alpha of course," Kellan smirked. Rita couldn't help laugh as they jerked her around trying to hug her. She seriously missed her pack. And when she looked at Jayce who was shifting his weight on his feet trying not to flip out because males were all over his mate, she couldn't help but smile further.

"Alright give her some space," Jayce finally spoke up taking her from Kellan's arms. He held onto her protectively.

"Go love on your own damn mate you and Tristan," Jayce said to Kellan. "And you Jaxson, I don't know go find some woman to love on and leave mine alone."

"Ha, ha very funny," Jaxson said flipping him the middle finger. A pair of footsteps sounded, coming into the large dining area. The she-wolf that Rita had pretended to fight off came towards them.

"You're saved," she smiled at Rita.

"Thank you for the warning about that wolf attacking us."

"No worries."

"My name is Mira," she said.

"Nice to officially meet you." Rita didn't know what it was, but there was something off about the way Mira was looking at her. It was as if she was reading Rita's thoughts. Both Rita and her wolf didn't like it. So she turned away from her.

"So, do I get a tour or something?" Rita asked.

"YES!" The she-wolves shouted at once. They grabbed onto her and quickly led her away. That left Mira and the rest of the guys standing around.

"You and your pack are welcome to stay," Kellan told Dell. With how small their pack was, Kellan was worried they might not survive for too long on their own, even with an alpha.

"Thank for your generosity," Dell nodded.

"Be sure to remember who you are alpha too," Jaxson said. Even though Dell was an alpha, Jaxson, Tristan, Jayce, and Kellan's wolves were all more dominant than him. But the wolves in Dell's pack were submissive, and that was why Dell could be their alpha. But in this circle, Dell was just barely submissive in the eyes of dominant wolves. When two alphas spent too long together, they started to butt heads. But Jaxson was reminding Dell that even if he was an alpha, he was only stronger than his own wolves.

"Heard you," Dell responded.

"All the she-wolves are off limits by the way," Jaxson added looking at Dell's wolves.

"Jax," Kellan said shaking his head. "Relax." Even though Jaxson was always the most chilled wolf, and loved to joke around and tease the others, when new wolves were introduced into their territory he became serious about being an enforcer. Essentially, Kellan granted them access to their territory, but it was Jaxson and Tristan who would enforce their way of life and rules.

"You can relax if you want to," Jaxson said. "But they've had one female in their pack, and now suddenly they're surrounded by she-wolves."

"They won't touch your she-wolves," Dell spoke up. "But Kyra isn't mated, so if-" Jaxson cut him off.

"Off limits," he said. "And if you or anyone of your wolves want Kyra you're gonna have to go through me to get her." Jaxson stood menacingly over them, and no one protested. Who would? Jaxson was dangerous, and they all knew that.

"Damn," Kellan said. "Welcome to matehood." Jaxson brushed him off.

"Don't talk crazy. She's not my mate."

"You sure as hell acting like it," Tristan commented.

"You don't get to judge me," Jaxson snapped.

"Me and Gemma have an understanding alright? So butt out of it."

"An understanding?" Jaxson gasped.

"I oughta slap the shit out of you for not mating that sweetheart. You sound dumb as fuck."

"How you giving me shit when it seems like you won't claim your own mate?"

"Because she's not my mate Tristan! We've all known Kyra forever. If she was my mate, I'm pretty sure I would have known way before now."

Jayce watched his pack mates go back and forth. Their talk about the imperfections of their mating reminded him that even though he'd found his mate, they hadn't completed the bond. But all that changed now. After losing her to Maverick, Jayce knew how important it was to complete the bond with Rita.

"I don't know why you giving me all the shit," Tristan said.

"Jay ain't mate with Rita." All three of them looked at Jayce.

"You should probably go take care of that," Kellan said.

"I agree," Tristan and Jaxson said at the same time. Jayce smiled and shook his head at his packmates as he walked away. He followed the scent of his mate surrounded by the other she-wolves of the pack. They were in Bliss and Kellan's room chatting. Jayce closed his eyes and knocked on the door.

"Get decent, man entering," he said. The females laughed.

"No one's naked," Gemma said. Jayce opened his eyes.

"Can I steal her from you all?" Jayce asked.

"Well, technically she is yours," Bliss sighed. "Go on, have her. We'll take her back tomorrow morning."

"Oh, I thank you so much my alpha." Jayce bowed sarcastically. Bliss threw a pillow at him.

"Get the fuck out," she laughed. Jayce smiled and took Rita's hand leading her out of the room and through the tunnels.

"You must be exhausted," he said to her.

"I am. But so happy to be here with my pack."

"I'm more than happy to have you back," Jayce told her. He walked with through the tunnels until he got to his room. He opened the door and let her walk in first.

"I'm not much of a designer, so it's pretty bare, but I figured you'd want to do all the designing yourself anyways." Rita looked at him with a confused look.

"You usually don't take my advice on much," she said. "Why would you do so now?"

"Well if this is our room then I would need your advice on some things no?"

"Ours?" Rita asked. She backed away from him.

"Yes ours," Jayce said. "I know you're not about to try and deny our mating."

"I'm not denying we're mates Jayce, but we didn't complete our mating bond for a reason."

"True that. But I watched you get kidnapped, Rita. And then I had to spend days without you. I went fucking nuts. And realizing how it was to be without you, I know I can't take for granted having you in my life." Rita crossed her arms and sighed hard. While being held captive, all she could think about was her mate, and she wanted him bad. But that didn't change the fact that they both wanted two different things.

"I don't mean to be a bitch about this Jay, but what changed?" she asked. "The fact that I was kidnapped?"

"Well, yes," he replied.

"What if I told you that's not enough?"

"Not enough?"

"I've been here Jayce," she said. "Before I was kidnapped I was here. You could have mated me at any point. But because I was kidnapped, now you realize you wanna complete the mating bond."

"You weren't necessarily making it easy for us to mate," Jayce said.

"And then you ran off to be with Kellan without even coming to me about it first."

"Well, you made it clear you had beta duties, and I didn't feel safe, so I had to find Kellan. In the end, I still got kidnapped, so it doesn't even really matter. We've had disagreements and arguments, and we barely spoke after I left to find Kellan."

"I know it hasn't been perfect, but I just want you."
Rita felt horrible to have him confess to her. Because even if
she could get over the fact that she didn't want to be a beta,
or that he wasn't ready to have pups, her being kidnapped in
the first place changed her. From the scars on her body to
knowing fact that she willingly gave herself to another wolf
even knowing she had a mate. If Jayce knew that about her,
he wouldn't be thrilled. She wasn't even thrilled with herself.
And he didn't say anything, but Rita could smell Maverick in
her pores, and she knew if she could smell it, so could he.
And it disgusted her. But there was no getting rid of his scent
because he'd marked her. And once Jayce found that out she
didn't know how she was going to save face.

"Can we talk about this another time? I need to get
some rest Jayce. I'm feeling weak."

"Yeah, yeah I understand. We'll discuss our living
arrangements later, but you can still spend the night with me.
I think both our wolves would very much appreciate it." Rita
shook her head tentatively. He couldn't see her naked.

"No, Jayce I-I just need to be alone for a little bit okay?" He didn't look happy not one bit, but he nodded. Rita felt like her heart was going to rip to pieces. Jayce's anger she could deal with. But his disappointment, and sorrow that she couldn't handle. Being a dominant wolf and still able to show emotions like that meant something. And before she broke down completely she hurried out of his room and traveled the tunnels until she got to the room she'd chosen earlier with the other she-wolves.

****

Rita was awake before the sun rose the next morning, unable to sleep any longer. She had reoccurring dreams of fucking Maverick and each time she woke she was physically ill. It was the worst feeling anyone could have to live with. She worried about facing her own pack mates knowing what she'd done for freedom, but she knew if she hid they wouldn't stop trying to investigate what was wrong with her. She'd showered over and over scrubbing her skin, but Maverick's scent didn't disappear. She didn't even know why she tried. She already knew it wasn't going to go away. Before she left her room to join the others, she dressed in a pair of jeans and a t-shirt. She didn't have scars on her arms, so she was thankful for that.

The chatter and laughter of her pack as she entered the dining area filled her up making her smile for the first time that day. Her night was restless, and hearing laughter made her feel better.

"Rita!" Amber, Maya, and Brandy screamed her name at the same time before launching onto her in a group hug. Rita fell to the ground under their weight laughing as they hugged and kissed her.

"I'm happy to see you too," she laughed as she wrestled them off her. She sat up with them on the floor checking their bodies to make sure they weren't injured.

"Are you guys alright?" Rita asked.

"Are you kidding? This place is fucking amazing!"

"Watch your mouth," Rita scolded hitting Amber playfully on the thigh. She stood and brought them up with her.

"You know, we're not kids," Maya added.

"Well you're a kid to me," Rita said ruffling her hair.

"What's for breakfast?" She walked towards the dining table and greeted the rest of the pack. She tried to smile and appear normal, but when she looked at Jayce, he did not smile at her. She felt so stupid trying to hide something she knew she couldn't hide, but she made sure her sister locks hide Maverick's bite mark and sat down next to Gemma. Everyone passed food down to her to make sure she got enough of everything.

"We were thinking that after our pack run we take you to the hot springs on the other side of the mountain. Just the ladies," Bliss said. Rita paused between eating. If she went on a pack run, at the end when she shifted back to human everyone would see her scars because she'd be naked. Getting in the hot sprints sounded relaxing as well, but there was the issue of her scars again. But how much could she deny doing with her pack? She decided it was easier to hide from half the pack instead of all of them.

"I'm still a little tired, I didn't get that much sleep," she finally spoke. "So I'll pass on the pack run. But I'd love to go to the springs."

"Sounds like a plan," Bliss smiled at her. Rita smiled and looked at everyone else. The males gave her small smiles that could be more or less grimaces more than smiles, but Jayce didn't give her anything. Rita just looked away from him and continued to eat her breakfast. The rest of the pack chatted quietly. Rita was beginning to wonder how they were going to deal with Maverick and she had to come clean about what it is Maverick wanted her to do and why he'd ultimately set her free. But seen as no one was going to bring it up she didn't want to.

She stayed quiet and ate her breakfast listening to the rest of them talk. After breakfast, while everyone else went for the pack run Rita stayed alone in the cave and cleaned up the dishes from breakfast. For the moment she could relax because no one was around her and she didn't have to be conscious about her body around her pack. After she finished cleaning up, she went to her room. Her closet was filled with clothes she'd had at Kellan's cabin, plus some new ones. She had underwear and bras but no bathing suit. She just put on a long robe and waited for the females to come back.

After some time the she-wolves came knocking at Rita's door. They were dressed in two-piece bikinis. Bliss was carrying some bathing suits in her hands.

"I knew you didn't have any and when we went shopping for more clothes after we moved in, we didn't buy you any. But I have extra you can choose from," Bliss said. They all walked in the room, and Rita closed the door behind them. Bliss spread the bathing suits out on the bed and Rita chose the one piece. It would most cover up the scars on her stomach and back, but the ones on her thighs would be out.

"How was the run?" Rita asked.

"Refreshing as always," Gemma replied. "Sucks you didn't come with us."

"The males can't see me naked. Especially Jayce," Rita said.

"You were always comfortable with nudity," Bliss gasped. "You were the one that told me to get comfortable with it!" Rita sighed and undid her robe and let it fall to the ground. She kept Maverick's mark covered with her hair but showed them everything else. All at once gasps filled the room, but after that, it was complete silence. As the alpha female, Bliss was the first to speak.

"This does not make you any less beautiful," she spoke fiercely.

"If you don't want to flaunt it, we all understand, but we won't think differently of you or shame you for it. You're a she-wolf of the Phoenix pack, and we're all bad bitches." Rita smiled and hugged her alpha female. She felt the love thriving between the bond their shared, and it truly built Rita up. She needed it now more than ever.

"We won't say a word to the guys, but you should talk to Jayce about it. He is your mate after all," Kyra told her.

"I know," Rita sighed.

"It'll just take me some time." Amber, Maya, and Brandy hugged Rita at the same time. They were wearing bathing suits that each pack member had let them borrow.

"She got those scars because of us," Amber told them somberly.

"Protecting and defending us."

"You're an amazing wolf," Gemma said.

"This is a setback, and you might feel crappy about how you look, but none of us view you any differently other than you're even more a badass than before."

"Thanks girls," Rita sniffled.

"I needed that. Now I think I need to see these hot springs."

"Get ya sexy ass in the bathing suit and we will," Bliss said spanking her playfully. Rita excitedly put on the bathing suit relieved to have something off her chest. It was better to have her sisters knowing her secrets than no one knowing at all. After she put on the bathing suit, she put on the robe to keep herself covered until they got to the springs. Mira had changed into a bathing suit as well, but she'd joined them in the kitchen once they were all dressed, so she hadn't seen Rita's scars. And Rita didn't know how she felt about the she-wolf in the first place, so she wasn't going to share a secret with her around.

"Damn!" Jaxson nearly dropped his bottle of beer when the she-wolves came into the living area ready for the hot springs. At some point, he'd seen all his packmates naked, but it was different when they wore sexy clothing. It added sexuality to them. He didn't want to view any of his packmates like that, and he didn't. But when he looked at Kyra, he couldn't help himself. It was unusual. And then when he looked at Mira; he felt a pull. She smiled seductively at him, but Jaxson looked away immediately. Even if he was more dominant than Dell, he wasn't going to disrespect him by looking at his she-wolf in any way that wasn't platonic. He quickly snapped out of his daze, to the smell of a male wolf's arousal. He looked at one of Dell's wolfs who was glaring at Gemma. Jaxson nudged Tristan and nodded to the wolf. Tristan got up immediately and went over to the wolf. He whipped out his claws and grabbed the wolf around his neck.

"What you looking at?" Tristan growled in his ear.

"No-nothing," he replied shakily.

"Take your eyes off my mate my dude. I catch you looking at her again I'll rip your fucking eyes out and make you swallow them." He dug his claws into his neck for added effect before he let him go.

"Get out of here Gemma," Tristan ordered. Dell's wolves deliberately looked up at the ceiling as all the she-wolves walked by them, not wanting to cause any of the dominant wolves to confront them about looking at their she-wolves. Kellan smacked Bliss on the ass as she walked by. They shot each other heated looks with promises of special activities later on in the day that Rita took notice to. She felt jealousy not towards Kellan or Bliss, but jealousy in just wanting her mate and wanting to give her all to him. She just wished there was no complication. She wished they could just mate and their fairytale would start. But fairy tales weren't real.

The hot springs was earth's natural Jacuzzi. When Rita sunk down into the warm liquid embedded within the cavern of the mountain on the other side she was in pure heaven. She made sure her hair hid the bite mark on her shoulder as she relaxed into the water. Bliss popped a bottle of champagne and passed around glasses. For the young wolves Bliss gave them some apple cider.

"How come Gemma gets champagne?" Amber asked.

"Gemma is 18," Bliss replied.

"Technically we went through puberty by shifting. So, really we're adults."

"Nice try," Bliss smiled.

"We can have pups and bleed but can't have a glass of champagne," Maya teased.

"Wait, she-wolves have periods?" Bliss asked. Everyone laughed at her.

"Of course we have periods," Gemma replied. "We're still females. We just don't bleed every month." Rita looked at Bliss with a questioning look.

"You didn't bleed after you went into heat?" Rita asked her.

"No. Was I supposed to?"

"When human females bleed that's just their body releasing the egg that could have been fertilized. We don't bleed often because we only bleed after our heating cycle because the heating cycle is the only time we can reproduce. So after we go into heat either we're pregnant or we bleed," Rita told her.

"I bled after my heating cycle. And I knew it was coming. Not like my mate fucked me," Gemma sighed shaking her head.

"So wait? Am I pregnant right now?" Bliss shrieked. All the she-wolves leaned into Bliss and sniffed.

"No," they all said at the same time.

"Wait? You can smell pregnancy?" Bliss asked.

"Yeah. There's little wolves can't smell," Mira told her.

"And if you were pregnant Bliss it would show. It won't be like a human pregnancy. It doesn't take five months to show you're carrying."

"How long does it take?"

"Matter of days," Kyra said.

"Our babies develop for only about two months before we give birth. Thankfully. That nine-month shit is ridiculous," Kyra laughed.

"Wow!" Bliss was in shock. "So what does it mean that I went into heat but didn't bleed, and I'm not pregnant? And trust me Kellan fucked me. He fucked me good."

"You're gonna go into heat again," Mira said confidently.

"How the hell do you know that?" Rita asked.

"Oh, I don't think anyone's told you," Mira started. "I'm an empath. Meaning I can feel other people's emotions, take them away or sometimes make them feel something else. My mother was a native American who passed the gift to me and help me hone it in. I wouldn't say I can predict the future, but I read aura's that help me learn things about someone, and I just get strong feelings about them. Sometimes I'm wrong, sometimes I'm right. But this time I know for a fact that you're gonna go into heat again Bliss."

"Well when? That shit hurt like a bitch! I need to get prepared!"

"I don't know when. It's just in the near future."

"Having that power doesn't drive you crazy?" Kyra asked her. Mira shrugged.

"Sometimes it does, but then it comes in handy. I always know when someone is being genuine or when they're keeping secrets." Mira looked at Rita as she said that. Rita just rolled her eyes and looked away.

"Not everyone's life is an open book," Bliss spoke up immediately noting the shot that Mira took at Rita. "And just because it's a secret to you doesn't mean it's a secret to anyone else. And hell, if it's a secret to you in the first place, maybe it's not your right, or your place to know their business." Mira looked at Bliss feeling her contempt.

"So you can read aura's right?" Bliss asked. "What can you read about mine right now?" Mira looked at her before inhaling and exhaling.

"Agitation, annoyance."

"Good so you know." Kyra and Gemma chuckled as Bliss continued to dig into Mira.

"Are you thinking you can take me in a fight?" Mira gasped. "I was born a shifter! I hardly think you can beat me. And I don't want to embarrass the alpha female in front of her wolves."

"Right, I am not a born shifter. But my mate taught me certain shit. I may be a new wolf, but I know my strength. And well, I don't mean to be a bitch about it but point blank I'm stronger than you. And I can make your wolf submit to me, Mira. So you can try me if you want to." Mira was quiet.

"Kellan has invited you and your pack to stay with us," Bliss said. "And while you're here you're going to respect all my sister wolves. Or I'm just gonna beat the shit out of you. Your choice."

Gemma and Kyra lost control of their chuckles and giggles that turned into full-on cackles of laughter. Even the young wolves began laughing, but they were trying to be subtle about it. Rita cracked a smile at Bliss and winked at her before mouthing *thank you.* Bliss winked backed at her.

The rest of the time in the hot springs Mira was quiet but the rest of the she-wolves laughed and chatted about everything under the moon. Only when the champagne bottle was empty did they gather their things and leave earth's Jacuzzi. Back inside the cave, everyone went to their rooms to get changed. Rita was the first out of her room once she changed into jeans and another t-shirt. Kellan was sitting in the living room on the large couch deep in thought.

"Hey Kell," Rita greeted. She sat on the opposite chair not wanting to sit next to him. He snapped from his thoughts and looked at her with a smile.

"What's up girl? How was the springs?"

"It was amazing. I needed it," she replied. He nodded at her.

"Where's Jayce?"

"Working out with Jaxson and Tristan. He's on edge for some reason so working out is the best thing for him right now."

"Oh." Rita knew why her mate was on edge. It had to be the fact that she smelled like Maverick. It was strange because she knew everyone could smell the change in her scent but no one was saying anything about it.

"We're gonna have a meeting about Maverick," Kellan spoke.

"Even though he let you go he's still out there and a danger to all she-wolves and smaller packs."

"Yeah, he is," Rita replied. The other wolves began filtering into the kitchen and the dining area. Rita and Kellan joined them. Jaxson and Tristan were there, but Jayce still wasn't around. They smelled freshly showered, so she knew they were done with their workout.

"What do you suppose we do about Maverick now?" Dell questioned sipping on a beer. "I feel highly uneasy that he's just free."

"I'm sure we all feel that way," Kellan said.

"But it was either his freedom or Rita's life. And I easily made my decision."

"Sometimes sacrifices need to be made for the greater good," Dell said. Kellan gave him a face.

"Shut your superhero sounding ass up," Kellan snapped. "Greater good my ass."

"Well, now it's gonna be a wild goose chase to find him again. How do you plan on even finding him huh?"

Rita felt her heart begin to beat faster in her chest. She should have told Kellan from jump why Maverick had let her go and what he wanted her to do. But then it would come to question why Maverick trusted her. And then she'd have to admit what she'd done to earn his trust. She wasn't proud of it. And even speaking it to the she-wolves was embarrassing. That's why she hadn't told them.

"Don't worry about how we're gonna find him," Kellan was glaring at Dell his eyes beginning to flash wolf so Dell would know he was treading on thin ice.

"Or we could just ask her," Mira spoke up pointing at Rita. Everyone was confused.

"Excuse me?" Kellan asked.

"She's keeping secrets!" Mira accused. Anger and embarrassment filled Rita, threatening to combust. Mira had some nerve to call her out like that in front of the pack. But before Rita could defend herself, Bliss was growling with a mouth full of canines.

"You really wanna go there?!" Bliss shrieked. Without giving Mira a chance to answer, Bliss was flying at her, all claws and teeth ready for a fight. Being less dominant, Mira squealed and ran behind Dell hiding behind her alpha. Dell pumped his chest out ready to push Bliss away from Mira, but Kellan stepped in. He grabbed Bliss by the arm and pushed her behind him before glaring down at Dell.

"Wrong one," Kellan growled. "Back the fuck up." Dell backed down without a question.

"I'm just trying to keep them from fighting," Dell said.

"Your alpha female can't just attack my less dominant female."

"Yeah well, she needs to learn to shut her mouth! I already warned her about taking shots at any of the wolves here. So clearly she wants to challenge me."

"It's not my fault she's keeping secrets! Go on, ask her what she'd hiding!"

"She doesn't have to prove herself to you!" Bliss snapped. "Just who the fuck do you think you are?!"

"I'm the only one willing to call on the truth here! Everyone knows something is up, and no one wants to speak on it, but I will! Tell us what's going on Rita!" She shouted.

"Yes Rita, tell us." Jayce's menacing voice came from behind her. Rita jumped and turned around to see her mate breathing down her neck. She was panicking so much she hadn't heard or scented him come up behind her.

"Jayce," she breathed.

"You're gonna let her hassle your mate like that?" Bliss gasped.

"I just want answers," Jayce replied not breaking eye contact with Rita. He stepped forward, but Rita only backed up.

"I wanna know," Jayce gritted. "Why you've taken showers, and I can smell soap on you; you've been in the hot springs, but yet still all I can smell when I come near you is Maverick's scent. We all can fucking smell it, but no one wanted to give you a hard time. But I find it fucking hard to ignore now Rita. So Mira says you're hiding something. What the fuck are you hiding?" Rita just shook her head her words unable to form in her head, therefore, nothing came out of her mouth. What was she going to say?

"Out with it!" Jayce yelled. Bliss rushed over and stood between Rita and Jayce. She pushed Jayce back.

"Get off her back Jayce! She's been held captive by a lunatic, but you wanna be here giving her more grief. So what if she has a secret. She doesn't have to tell you shit!"

"Bliss, move," Jayce said. "This is between me and my mate."

"He's right Bliss," Kellan spoke up. He took Bliss by the arm and pulled her away softly.

"Jayce please," Rita begged. "The scent it'll go away I just don't know how long and-"

"Rita help me out here," Jayce pleaded. "I'm losing my fucking mind. I'm craving you in a way I can't even begin to comprehend. I've always wanted a place in your life despite our differences. Just tell me. Please." Rita exhaled a shaky breath. She looked around at her entire pack before looking back at the desperateness in Jayce's eyes. After that, she just knew it she couldn't hide it anymore. Unable to look at him Rita pushed her sister locks back and away from her shoulder to show him Maverick's claiming bite. The air seemed sucked out of the cave at her reveal. Rita brought her eyes slowly towards Jayce. He was standing stoically, his chest rising and falling faster with each breath. He looked between her and the mark his eyes flashing rapidly between his human eyes and his wolf eyes.

"You-I don't understand," he spoke, his voice a deep growl and almost inhuman.

"I'm sorry," Rita whispered. Jayce pressed the heel of his hands against his temple as if his head was about to explode. He hunched over, his canines filling his mouth. Kellan pushed Rita back while the other male wolves stood in front of the she-wolves. It was evident Jayce was about to go feral. But she saw Jayce try and control himself.

"Alpha. Beta. Omega," he growled with his heels still pressed to his temple. He blinked his eyes and repeated the mantra over and over, but his wolf still continued fight. Hating to see her mate in that kind of turmoil, Rita skirted from behind Kellan and went over to Jayce.

"Rita no!" Kellan shouted. But it was already too late. Rita was in front of Jayce holding his face trying to talk to him.

"Come back to me," she whispered. He locked eyes with her, and for a moment they were human. Rita thought she'd gotten through to him but then his eyes went back wolf and he growled at her. With movements faster than she could track, he ripped her arms from him and twisted them. Rita squealed in pain, and he immediately let her go. With him towering over her Rita fell back, falling on her ass. He pounced on her, pushing her flat on the ground with his hand on her chest. Rita tapped into his head and heard a barrage of thoughts, but it was all geared to his hurt. He was past just being hurt. He was crushed. His wolf pushed through his human features giving him a snout. Jayce growled down in her face looking as if he wanted to end her life right then and there through all his pain. Rita wished he would. She wanted him to end it all for her. But something gave him restraint. He bellowed in her face before backing off. His muscles began to shift under his skin. A howl ripped from his lungs as he went into shift. He raced away running as fast as he could to get out of the cave.

"Follow him!" Kellan ordered Tristan. Tristan immediately ran after Jayce to make sure he didn't go rogue and be lost to the pack both physically and mentally. Rita watched Tristan leave, sitting up slowly. Tears streaked down her face as defeat filled her. She looked at everyone around her, and they all wore solemn expressions, and no one could figure out what to say. And then Rita looked at Mira. Fury and hatred bled through her defeat. Even if she didn't want to tell anyone about her bite she knew she would have to. But Mira took the choice of *when* to come clean to her pack away from her. And that's what was pissing Rita off. She had yet to release her wolf since she'd been back and right at that moment seemed to be a perfect time. Rita didn't have a slow burn of her emotions. She didn't let it stew or even think about her attack. One moment she was sitting there crying, and the next her claws and canines were out and ready to attack. She launched herself at Mira and just inches from her claws connecting to Mira's skin Rita felt herself being held back.

"Let me go!" Rita screamed, almost begging to get her hands on Mira.

"None of this is my fault!" Mira shouted. "It was your secret!"

"Who gives you the right!" Rita cried out. "Maverick gave me *hell*. Jayce is my mate and anything to further split us apart *kills* me. And you think being claimed by another wolf is something I want to reveal to everybody? You don't think that maybe I just wanted to come clean to my mate in private? Who the fuck do you think you are huh?" Mira continued to hide behind Dell not saying a word. She had a reason to hide. The other she-wolves were being affected by Rita's anger. Amber, Maya, and Brandy had their claws out and were growling. Their agitation triggered Gemma and Bliss and whereas Kyra was the more wolf in control even she was ready to fight.

Kellan saw the massacre about to happen and wanted to put an end to it immediately before it got well out of control. He turned to his she-wolves and blared his alpha vibes onto them seemingly crushing them with his power until their wolves submitted and backed off. Bliss was the only wolf that was left standing, but her wolf was subdued.

"Are we calm?" Kellan asked. Each wolf nodded. He let go of Rita. She didn't go for the attack again, but her anger and loathing didn't dwindle.

"Kellan," she snapped. "I am your wolf. I am part of your pack. This newcomer or whatever the fuck she is has just violated me! As my alpha, you need to defend my honor! No one knows what the fuck I sacrificed for my freedom and their freedom," Rita pointed at Amber, Maya, and Brandy.

"And I'll be damned if this fucking fortune teller comes here and makes me out to be a betrayal to my pack."

"You're right Rita," Kellan said.

"She has violated you. But you should know that none of us think any different of you. I trust you with my life as I'm sure the rest of the pack does. Unfortunately, I am not her alpha. I cannot punish her. That duty lays with Dell." Kellan looked at Dell.

"But I will say if Mira is not punished for her actions today, I will have to ask your pack to leave our home. And I'm pretty sure you need our protection more than I need yours," Kellan said. Dell just gave a curt nod.

"Pack meeting tonight at ten," Kellan informed them. With that, he and Jaxson walked away talking about going to help Tristan handle Jayce.

"You're gonna have to do a hell of a lot to earn our trust again," Bliss spat at Mira.

"Come on girls." Bliss came over to Rita and took her hand. She put her arm around Rita's waist and led her away.

They went to Rita's room, and Rita sank into her bed. Her body was numb as her heart was in despair. Realizing she didn't know what else to do, Rita hid her face in her pillow and just wept.

Chapter Thirteen

Jayce was at a loss for words. His mate claimed by someone else. The one thing he was holding onto was the fact that he had put a mark on Rita. But that was completely drowned out by another wolf's mark and that's what undid Jayce. He paced back and forth in wolf form.

Do you think Rita would want him to mark her? Tristan asked in Jayce's mind. Tristan's wolf was sitting alertly watching Jayce pace.

I know she didn't want it. But I can't control how my wolf feels. How I feel. Imagine marking Gemma, and some other wolf had the audacity to mark her too. The universe gave her to me. Not to Maverick, not anyone else. Me.

You know it would be just like Maverick to mark any female he captures. He's sick in the fucking head.

Your mate needs you. Kellan came into the clearing in wolf form with Jaxson next to him. Jayce turned and looked at his alpha.

I know how hard it may be to control your emotions or even think straight. But just look inside yourself and feel your mate's need for you. What Maverick did was fucked up. And we're gonna get him for it that's for damn sure. But in the time being, you cannot let your relationship with Rita further crumble. Kellan's words rang true. It was all fucked up, but all Jayce should focus on was trying to heal with his mate. She'd been through too much already. Hell, he'd even almost attacked her in all his rage. Jayce stopped pacing and searched himself for his mate. He felt the wetness of her tears and knew immediately she was crying.

I want to go to her but I know I won't be able to control my animal, Jayce admitted. Just like earlier in the day the moment he could still smell Maverick on her he felt like tearing shit up. No doubt if he went back and scented Maverick on his mate again his control was going to fall apart again.

I have silver cuffs back at the entrance of the cave. It'll take away your powers, and your senses will be human, and it will quiet your wolf, Kellan said. Jayce showed his compliance to the plan by beginning to walk back towards their home. He'd ran for only about two miles before he stopped to gather himself.

Heading back to the cave, everyone was quiet. Jayce continued to feel how his mate needed to be comforted and that further helped him to see how much she did need him. His reaction wasn't something he could control, but thinking about it he wished he hadn't had that outburst. The last thing he wanted was for Rita to be afraid of him.

Before going beyond the metal door in the cave, all four of them shifted and dressed in the clothes that Kellan had set at the entrance before he went to find Jayce and Tristan. Jayce just pulled on his jeans and stood waiting for the cuffs to come.

"We're only doing this because we want you to have control just to be around your mate. But I don't want to keep them on for too long. Once we find Maverick, I need you at your best strength. And as Beta, you have duties regarding the three young wolves. We have to reconnect them with their pack." Jayce nodded.

"Once I handle this with Rita I'll get to my duties."

"Good," Kellan nodded. "We'll give you space to do what you need to do. But just remember that not everything will fix itself in one day."

"I know," Jayce sighed. He winced as the power of his animal was trapped within him as Kellan applied the cuffs. It took him several breaths to keep composure of himself during the draining of his power. But once it was done, he headed straight to see Rita. Even though he hated keeping his wolf trapped, having the cuffs on served a very convenient purpose for the time being.

In Rita's room, all the she-wolves were gathered on her bed talking with her softly. When he appeared in the doorway, all eyes turned to him. He showed his silver cuffs so they knew he wouldn't be losing control. The room was dark, and Rita was tucked under the covers wearing a t-shirt that was bigger than her body and covered her completely. Jayce noticed that it was his shirt.

"Sorry, I went through your things to get it," Gemma said.

"She needed it."

"It's alright," Jayce replied. At hearing his voice, Rita turned around sharply and looked at him. He gave her a weak smile.

"Excuse me, ladies," Jayce said to them. They all smiled at him and left the room, sending him positive vibes through their pack bond. Once they were gone, Jayce closed Rita's door and walked over to her bed. She scooted over and made space for him to sit on the edge. He rubbed her thigh over the sheets in a comforting gesture.

"I'm sorry I attacked you the way I did," he said. "Are you alright?"

"Yes," she whispered. "How-how come-" Jayce showed her the silver cuffs knowing she was going to ask why he wasn't bugging the fuck out anymore.

"Oh," she nodded.

"I know you didn't ask Maverick to mark you, and he's egotistic enough to think if he marks all the females he kidnaps then he's some sort of supreme ruler. It was wrong of me to take my anger out on you."

"I know you didn't mean to attack me," she said. "I saw you struggling with restraint."

"Does your wolf...does she see me as her mate still or is she loyal to Maverick?" Jayce asked tentatively.

"Oh god no. She despises Maverick. When he marked me, I had on silver cuffs, but she tried hard to get out and attack him. Even with his scent on us, we know who our mate is."

"While I have on these silver cuffs it's probably best we talk about our future," Jayce said.

"You know we have to complete the bond. Or else we're going to be in pain. Unless of course, we keep marking each other, but at some point, it just won't be enough. My wolf already feels disrespected because you were marked by someone else. So what he's going to want is a full bond that no one can take away from us once it's completed."

"My wolf wants to complete the bond too. And well, so do I."

"But obviously there's some things in our way huh?" Jayce asked. Rita nodded.

"Move over," he said pushing the sheet aside so he could get in next to her. Because the t-shirt she was wearing covered her scars, she was okay with him coming into the bed next to her. And then there was the fact that it was dark in the room and at the moment his vision was human. They laid facing each other.

"Being a beta is all I've ever wanted," Jayce said to her.

"Growing up, my best friend was the son of the alpha, and I just knew I was never going to be an alpha. I mean, I'm strong enough for it but with the connection me, Tristan, Jax, and Kellan had we already knew what positions we would have. And it's what we've done now. I followed around the beta's of the pack all through my childhood, and when Kameron made me beta, it was the best day of my life. This isn't just a job you know. It's who I am. Just as mush as Kellan is an alpha."

"That's why I would rather not mate than to have you leave your position. At first, I thought you would, and it was wrong of me to suggest that you should step down. I don't want to take anything from you."

"Not having you takes something away from me Rita. You have to know that."

"But what about me wanting a pup? That's not something you want."

"Because I don't want you to feel as if I'm neglecting our pup because I'm fulfilling beta duties. And if we're going to be the beta couple a pup could always complicate things."

"I never knew my parents," Rita sighed.

"I grew up as an orphan. I had a pack, but none of the members took care of me or wanted me around. My alpha, he didn't tell me anything about my parents. So I slept outside didn't have a home and I ended up eating scraps the other wolves tossed out." Even though his wolf was subdued, that didn't stop the animal from feeling anger at the way his mate was treated.

"When I hit puberty and shifted for the first time there was no one to help me along. No one to guide me through the shift."

"What about your heating cycle? After you shifted?"

"I just dealt with it," she said.

"Every time I went into heat I dealt with it. But after my first shift, the alpha wanted to make me his mistress or fuck buddy or whatever you wanna call it. His mate was not happy and thought that I was the one trying to fuck her man so being part of the alpha pair, she banished me from the pack. And I was only 17. I was an omega until I stumbled upon Kameron's pack and found you."

"I can't believe it," Jayce shook his head.

"I always endured the pain of my heat cycle because I knew that because I didn't have anyone who cared for me, or who loved me or called me family, I would one day want my own. I'd find my mate who'd love me to the end of time, and we'd have pups that I could love and show them what it means to help others and be kind. I couldn't risk fucking anyone during my cycle and ending up with a pup to someone who didn't love me." Jayce was beginning to understand why she thought nothing else of her future but having pups because she didn't have family, to begin with.

"I just find it crazy how you were able to survive being an omega since you were 17 Rita. That's fucking incredible. It makes me so proud that I have a mate as strong as you." Doubt crept into Rita's body. Yes, he was complimenting her on her strength. But instead of fighting her way out of Maverick's clutches, she gave up on that and decided to just fuck the man instead. What would he think of her if he knew that?

"I'm not that strong," she sighed. Jayce pushed her locks from her face. Laying there and looking into her beautiful face he was tempted to do much more than to just lay with her. Leaning forward he pressed a small kiss to her lips.

"I've been longing to have you again ever since our first time," he commented.

"Me too," she agreed. "I've fucked before, but you were the only male that gave me true pleasure. Now I know why my wolf wanted me to find your pack in the first place."

"What do you mean?"

"I was wandering around the woods in wolf form, and for some reason, my animal wouldn't let me pass Kameron's territory without coming onto it. She took control and led me to Kameron. And now I know why. She felt that her mate was near."

"That wolf of yours brought us together," Jayce smiled.

"And we should have never let our differences take us apart." Jayce ran his thumb over her plump lips.

"Mate with me," he whispered. "So I don't have to wear silver when I'm around you." Rita felt a sense of panic. There should be nothing holding her back from completing the bond with her mate. But she felt so unsure. So afraid of the secrets she had yet to show him or tell him. There was still also the fact that she didn't want to take the role of beta. She wanted to orient herself around being a mother.

"You know how I feel about being beta. And I don't want to hold you back either."

"Well then let me mark you again until we figure it out. But I need to do something." Rita sensed his need, and it only hiked up her own need. Since they were already so close together, Rita didn't have to lean far to kiss him. He was ready to ravish her lips sending fire and desire ripping through her body. Her nipples hardened beneath his t-shirt. When he went to grab her ass under the shirt, Rita stopped him, fearful that he would feel the raised scars on her body. Distracting him from why she didn't want him to touch her, Rita grabbed his growing erection. She quickly undid his jeans so she could pop him out of its confines. He was large and engorged in her hand, and for a moment she wanted to chicken out. But then she remembered the feeling of Maverick entering her body. She shivered in disgust. The only thing she wanted to remember was the feeling of her mate. That's it.

"I want all of you," she whispered as she rubbed his large erection.

"The keys to the cuff are in my pocket," he said knowing what she meant. He kissed her neck, trailing kisses along her collarbone. While she shimmied out of her underwear, he fished for the keys in his pocket. Rita was going to throw the panties off the bed, but Jayce grabbed it and held it against his nose. He inhaled before moaning in pleasure. Rita understood what he was doing. He needed her scent almost overpowering anything else, or he would lose control. Thankfully the honey dripping from her insides at just his kisses had pooled in her panties before she'd taken them off. Her fresh arousal would smell nothing like Maverick.

He pressed the flimsy material of her panties to his nose with one hand, and used his other hand to delve into her honey slicked folds to prepare her for his entry. Moaning, and humming in delight, Rita unlocked the silver cuffs. The cuff around the wrist of the hand that was fingering her insides, she took longer to uncuff. She couldn't quite concentrate as he was digging inside of her, making her gush fluids. But she successfully got the cuffs off him. His wolf eyes came to life, glaring down at her. Rita was unsure how much of Maverick he could still smell, and the growl that he let out made her apprehensive. He threw her panties to the side, pulled his fingers from her folds and yanked her by the hip close to him. She raised her leg, draping it over his hip as his erection searched for her opening. His claws were digging into her hips, making holes in the t-shirt that allowed for his claws to embed into her skin.

He teased her opening, fucking her with his tip before he slammed himself home. Rita felt her eyes light up with the power of her wolf. Feeling her mate inside her brought her to immediate release. She shivered as she came hard. Jayce pulled her close and rested his forehead against hers locking stares with her.

"Even better than I remembered," Jayce groaned. His hips took on a life of its own pumping within his mate's tight cavern of honey. He could feel her muscles clamping all around him as she continued to orgasm. They kissed each other sloppily. Jayce felt like he couldn't get enough of her. He pumped harder and harder, and still, he wanted more. He wanted the pleasure to be never-ending. But both him and his wolf was strung too tightly. There was no way he was going to last any longer. His balls tightened ready to help shoot out his release. Since his claws were still digging into her hips, Jayce dragged them along her skin deep enough to mark her. the magical bond inside them started to knit together, but Jayce kept his bite to himself causing the bond to tear apart.

She wasn't ready to complete the bond, and even if it made Jayce upset, he wasn't going to rush her into making that type of decision. Their mating had to be without question. Rita let out a soul-shattering scream of ecstasy. Having him mark her and fuck her intensely made her succumb to a back-breaking orgasm. Jayce let out his own shout as his hips bucked. He jammed himself deep within her as his release began spurting out of him. For only a second a scene flashed in his head. It was the image of Rita round with his pup inside her, and then the picture was gone. Jayce never experienced that before but seeing the image made him actually think about having pups with his mate. Yes, he wanted them to be the powerful beta couple they were but at the same time, he wanted to have little shifter babies that would carry their mother's good looks, strength, and intelligence.

Both of them were breathing heavily as they looked at each other. Jayce's erection slowly died out, but he never withdrew from her body. He took a deep breath and exhaled a sigh of relief. Maverick's scent was no longer attached to her skin. Jayce couldn't help but nuzzle her neck finally feeling some sense of content.

"I'm going to fill your belly with as many pups as I can," Jayce whispered. "I'll give you the family you desire. All because I love you." Rita couldn't even breathe. How do you respond to something like that? How do you even begin to thank someone for being willing to give you what you want to make you happy?

"Jayce I-"

"It's alright," he hushed her.

"I know the beta position scares you, but we will figure it out. Because I'm not letting you go. Not this time. Understand?" Rita just nodded. "Use your words," he ordered softly.

"I understand," Rita spoke. He kissed her on the nose satisfied at her answer. He tried to caress her by putting his hand under the t-shirt. Panicking, Rita backed off separating their bodies. She climbed out of the bed quickly creating more separation. Jayce sat up and looked at her, suspicion painted on his expression. But instead of asking any questions he got out of the bed and fixed his clothing.

"I have to go and help Kellan get contact with the girls' alpha, he said speaking of Maya, Amber, and Brandy. Then we have a pack meeting." Rita nodded wrapping her arms around herself. Jayce didn't like how reserved his mate had become. He was so used to her speaking his mind her new attitude threw him. But being kidnapped was no easy situation. Things probably happened that changed her.

"Rita," he called. She vaguely looked at him.

"Look me in the face," he ordered. This time she brought her eyes directly to his.

"I'm not going to pretend that I can even comprehend the shit that you went through with Maverick. I'm also not here to judge you for whatever happened either. I'm here to support you. Because nothing changes the fact that I'm your mate. Nothing changes the fact that I'm ready to spend my life with you. You're a strong woman Rita. You've got attitude, and you speak your mind. Don't let anyone take that away from you. Not even me. Now come here and give me a kiss so I can go."

"You're gonna stop ordering me around," she said as she walked up to him. He cracked smile.

"Now that's the mate I remember." He wrapped his arm around her waist and kissed her softly. "I'm not done with you yet either, so I'll be back after the pack meeting."

"Are you telling me or asking me huh?" she teased.

"I think I need to get further in them guts to be satisfied. Plus, I lasted like 2 minutes. I don't want you walking around here thinking your mate ain't shit but a two-minute man. I can't have that on my conscience." He pecked her on the lips then turned and left the room without saying anything else. Rita was speechless as a warmness filled her stomach. A smile crept on her lips as she felt her cheeks heating. She felt like she was a teenager experiencing her first crush. But that's how being mated was supposed to feel right? Without a doubt, she loved Jayce. And she listened to his words. She just hoped he meant what he said about not thinking of her any differently. Because she'd yet to tell him what she done, or showed him her scars.

She appreciated his words about her character. It made her believe that although she went through the shit, she did with Maverick, she still came out on top. Or well, she was free. And she'd just been able to share her body with her mate. And that was something precious to her. Knowing Kellan and Jayce were busy handling business. Rita dressed and hurried over to Bliss's bedroom. Kellan was leaving the room when Rita arrived, but he didn't notice her since he was already through the tunnels.

"Hey Bliss," Rita said knocking on the door.

"Come in!" Bliss sang. Rita entered the bedroom and was hit with the aroma of sex. Kellan and Bliss's scents mingled together in the most perfect way that gave the aroma of their sex a fragrant smell. It was nothing like Hera and Maverick's scent. That was god awful. But Rita supposed sex between mates was fragrant because that was who you were meant to be with.

"Must be great fucking the alpha," Rita teased her. Bliss smiled.

"Great ain't even the word. And wait, I know you ain't talking shit coming in here smelling like Jayce's semen." Rita gasped.

"I do not!" She laughed. Bliss burst out laughing.

"That's what you get for teasing me." Rita shook her head and hopped into Bliss's bed.

"This is safe for me right?" Rita asked, looking around the bed to make sure she wasn't sitting in any body fluids.

"We didn't make it to the bed," Bliss smiled while winking. She joined Rita in bed. "Well you smell like Jayce for real, so that's a good thing?" she asked.

"He marked me to take away Maverick's scent. But we spoke about our mating."

"And?"

"If we complete the bond I'm going to become the beta. Much like you became the alpha female when Kellan mated with you. Only problem is that I know for certain we'll mate. We're born wolves, and we understand the importance of mating. Plus we don't want to be in pain."

"What's holding you back?"

"I don't want to be beta," Rita admitted.

"I always envisioned myself having a family, but the dynamic with Jayce changes things. I'm not interested in the politics of being beta. It's paperwork and full of tasks, and I'm not that kind of girl."

"Hm, I see," Bliss said. .

"It's not easy to have to take on something you don't want to or see yourself doing. But look at me. I'm a human turned shifter, and now I'm the alpha female of a pack. I could barely handle my own damn life much less the lives of shifters when I just became one myself. But like I've been learning the universe works in mysterious ways."

"I'm just worried I'll screw it all up. I've never been in a uniformed pack until now and when I first found Kameron's pack where I met Jayce and the guys. I've just always dreamt about having a family. Being with people who loved me and who I could love in return."

"Well can I ask you something?"

"Sure."

"Do you love Jayce?"

"Yes," Rita could answer without hesitation.

"If you love him then trust him to help you do right by the position. Plus, I think being beta is something he wants just as bad as you want kids. Is he willing to give you kids? Or pups, sorry the human in me," Bliss smiled.

"He told me he was moments ago in my room. He has no doubts about having pups even though its, not something he wanted at the moment."

"Relationships are sometimes made up of sacrifices Rita. Jayce is a good man. I don't want to see you lose him over a technicality. That, plus I think you're more of a beta than you realize." Rita stayed quiet, her thoughts enveloping her. Bliss saw her expression change with her deep thoughts and knew there was a lot she was considering.

"Wanna know something?" Bliss asked.

"What?"

"I'm not ready to have a pup."

"You're not?"

"Nope. But guess what? I'm going to make sure I have a pup. And soon."

"You are?" Rita was confused. Surely if Bliss wasn't ready for a pup, she shouldn't have one.

"Why? If you're not ready?" Rita asked.

"Because you want to have a pup," Bliss shrugged.

"And because my pack is depending on me and Kellan as alphas to start the growth of the pack. I'm not ready for a pup but I know having Kellan I'll have the best kind of support in this world. That plus I love my pack and will do what I need to. And it'll be cruel of me not to procreate so you can have a baby with your true love."

"Oh, Bliss." Rita leaned over and hugged Bliss tightly. Now Rita knew what she needed to do. It didn't matter if she didn't want to be beta. She had a mate that she needed to support just like he would support her. And Bliss showed her that sometimes love came with sacrifices. If she was going to have pups earlier than she planned for the sake of Rita being able to have her own baby. then there was nothing that should hold Rita back from committing to her mate. It was going to be hard, but she was going to show him her scars and tell him her secrets. If he accepted it, then she was going to complete the bond.

"Thanks so much," Rita said pulling away. "I understand now."

"Good," Bliss smiled.

"Where we having the pack meeting? There's much to discuss."

"We werent invited," Bliss scoffed.

"None of the she-wolves. Kellan says we can't fight with Maverick." Rita sucked her teeth.

"Well, I'll have Kellan know he has no hope of getting to Maverick without us. Come on let's get the other girls and crash that damn meeting. I oughta slap Jayce for tryna leave me out of it."

"Oh you're gonna be a great beta," Bliss laughed as she followed Rita out of the room.

Chapter Fourteen

Jayce walked into the meeting room after having a talk with the three young wolves. They could sense their alpha was still alive and thankfully it was the same pack where Gemma's parents had retired too so he could easily find them by getting in contact with Gabe and Gina. Kellan was inside the room looking over some papers when Jayce entered. Kellan looked up quickly not sure what kind of mood his friend would be in. Shock filled his features when he saw how relaxed Jayce was.

"Hey," Jayce greeted. Jaxson and Tristan looked at each other confused.

"Hey," all three wolves replied at the same time. Jayce noticed the looks his friends were giving him. He handed Kellan the silver cuffs.

"I think I'll be good without them," Jayce replied.

"Interesting," Kellan said. He leaned over and took a whiff of Jayce. He smelled of Rita, but their scents hadn't combined.

"We're not mated yet," Jayce said.

"But soon."

"So you're over the fact that the muthafucker marked your woman?" Tristan asked.

"No, I'm not over it. I'm still pissed. But she doesn't smell like him anymore. That's all I care about for the moment. Anyways, in other news, I talked to the girls about their alpha. He's still alive. I'll try the phone numbers I have for him, and if I get no response, I'll seek out Gabe and Gina." Tristan, Jaxson, and Kellan were at a loss for words at how Jayce was seemingly normal. For all this time he'd been struggling, and it was weird to see him the same normal guy again.

"I guess sex does fix a lot of shit," Jaxson commented. Jayce shot him a look.

"Shut it," he snapped with a smirk on his face.

"Are we going to get to the meeting or not?"

"Alright beta," Kellan smiled.

"Let's get to the meeting." They all sat around the table, but before they could even begin to speak, Kellan smelled the mixed scent of his mate along with the other she-wolves.

"Get ready for trouble," Kellan said just as the door opened and the ladies walked into the room. Bliss and Rita stood in front wearing determined looks on their faces.

"We demand that we be part of this meeting," Rita said.

"I already gave my orders on that. None of the she-wolves are to be included," Kellan replied.

"Well," Rita began. "Sorry for my disruption and you can punish me for my disrespect, but you can take your orders and shove it up your ass. We're gonna be part of this meeting because you have no hopes of getting near Maverick without our help." If it were anyone else talking to him like that, Kellan would have an outright display of his domination. But it was Rita. And she was a firecracker. She always spoke her mind, and Kellan loved it. So he couldn't help the smile that came to his face.

"Duly noted," he said nodding his head.

"Have a seat ladies." Bliss sat next to Kellan at the head of the table while the other wolves spread out. Jayce immediately stood and gave Rita his seat.

"Maverick wants pups by any she-wolf he can get his hands on. He even injected Hera with human medicine to speed up her heating cycle. I thought it was going to work, but then after a day her heat vibes just died out. But if he gets that kind of drug out there to any wolf, it can be dangerous. He has a very unlimited supply of wolfs bane, which is why it's imperative that we attack him from a different angle."

"What do you propose?" Kellan asked her. Rita noticed he was giving her the respect and authority of the beta position by even asking about her plans of attack. The alpha would only take consultation of those proportions by his beta and his mate of course.

"In order to escape I devised a plan which allowed Maverick to believe he had gotten me to see things his way. I basically shitted on you guys to get Maverick to believe me. Told him I wanted to be his alpha female and since Jayce wasn't claiming me, I wanted someone who would. That's why he bit me to mark me." The room was deathly quiet. Rita cleared her throat of her nerves. Jayce rubbed her shoulder softly giving her courage.

"He let me go not only to escape knowing you'd rather save me than attack him. But he also let me go because he wants me to set a trap for you all. Or more specifically the she-wolves. He knows that you'll trust me and he wants me to bring you to one of his clubs where he can effectively ambush us and kidnap you all."

"Seriously?" Kellan gasped.

"That's why I don't want any of the females part of this fight!"

"But this is exactly why we need to be part of this fight!" Rita countered.

"Kellan he thinks I'll be spoon feeding him she-wolves. Why don't I make it look like that's exactly what I'm doing? It won't be us walking into a trap. It'll be him. And let's face it, none of you are going to get close to him without getting shot full of wolfs bane." Rita sat back and crossed her arms. Kellan did the same. She could see the cold calculation in his eyes. He was not happy about this.

"We can do it," Gemma spoke up. Her voice was quiet but filled with determination.

"Yeah, we can," Kyra agreed. Kellan took a deep breath then turned and looked at his mate. She smiled at him, and they shared some intimate moment that no one was part of but them.

"Alright. Lay out the plans for us," Kellan said. None of the other wolves objected. Jayce smiled down at his mate. They were all there to support her and listen to her plan. Rita was drowning in support, and she couldn't even believe how incredible her pack was.

"When is this supposed to happen?" Kellan asked after Rita laid out her devised plan.

"One week," she replied.

"Jax and Tristan I want all the she-wolves trained. And I mean intensely. The skills you've taught them are good, but I want it multiplied. Train the young wolves as well. They're the future of their pack. They need to start learning some things. Got that?"

"Understood," Jaxson and Tristan said at the same time.

"What about Dell and his pack?" Jayce asked.

"I'll fill him in. Any last questions or comments?"

"Let's kill that muthafucker," Bliss said. Everyone snickered and laughed at their alpha female.

"Meeting adjourned," Kellan smiled. He put his arm around Bliss and kissed her on the cheek before walking with her out of the room.

"Good job," Jayce said once the room emptied leaving only him and Rita.

"Thanks," she smiled.

"Even though it's hard for me to let you go anywhere near Maverick again."

"Hell, it's hard for me to have to be near him too." Jayce noticed the shiver that ran through her body. It made Jayce wonder about certain things.

"He didn't touch you did he?" he questioned. Rita froze up at his question. She already committed to the fact that she was going to be telling him everything about her time with Maverick, but the task still scared her. If his reaction was going to be other than what she hoped for she'd be devastated.

"Touch me as in…?" Rita asked nervously.

"Sexually," Jayce replied giving her a look.

"I mean he marked you. Usually, markings happen during sex. I'm just hoping he wasn't having sex with you." Rita felt her devastation beginning to bloom. If he was already hoping Maverick hadn't touched her then how would he deal with the fact that Maverick had? And Rita had let him?

"Well did he?" Jayce growled at her. Rita snapped from her daze realizing she hadn't said anything for a moment.

"It shouldn't matter if he did or didn't," Rita finally said. "You were just fucking me it didn't seem to matter then."

"Well it does matter to me," he said. Rita shook her head. She knew then if she told him what happened then he would break her heart. She figured she could save herself the embarrassment and shame. Unfortunately, her heart was going to break if she told him the truth or if she didn't.

"So much for not judging me, and being here to support me, and what else was it you said? That nothing would change the fact that you want to spend the rest of your life with me? What sounded so good before now sounds like a load of bullshit," she breathed. "And to think I was ready to complete the mating bond with you." She shook her head before turning and leaving the room.

"What?" Jayce gasped not believing how quickly their relationship was breaking down after they'd only just built it back up. Not willing to just let it go that easily, Jayce hurried after Rita. She was halfway down the tunnel before he caught up to her.

"Wait, wait," he said grabbing her by the wrist. She turned around sharply and yanked her wrist from his hold.

"Don't touch me," she stated.

"What the hell Rita? All I said was that I hope he didn't touch you! You're my mate I wouldn't want anyone to touch you! And I'm sure you wouldn't want anyone to touch me either."

"You can fuck whoever you want to Jayce. I could care less."

"Seriously?" he questioned. "What in the hell changed Rita? I said I would be willing to have pups with you as soon as you wanted them. And I'm trying show you I love you. What else do you need from me?" Rita didn't have the answer to that question. She didn't know what she needed from him. She just knew that telling him what happened while he was in Maverick's captivity was nothing he would want to hear. Even if he did proclaim to want to support her, she just knew if he had this information it would be hard for him to view her the same.

"I guess I'm just not the same woman you knew from before. Being with Maverick changed me Jayce." She shrugged her shoulders backing away from him. "I thought we could just mate and be happy. But I'm starting to realize that maybe there's just some things that I can't get over. Maybe I can't help the fact that I've changed. So why drag you down with me?"

"Rita, please. Don't do this to me. I'm sorry if what I said upset you. Hear the truth in my words. Hear the truth by listening to my heartbeat. I'm not just gonna let you walk out of my life. A mated couple is only as strong as their weakest partner. Where you are weak Rita, I'm here to build you up. I'm here to strengthen you. To show you things about yourself that you can't believe for yourself. Without you Rita, I'm a weak man. I need you to feel strong. To feel like nothing in this world can stop me. I don't want to be weak Rita. That's what you can do for me. You can make me strong just like I can make you strong. Hell, I just don't want to be without you. Please don't make me live without you."

A single tear streaked down her face before her eyes flooded over and it rained tears. She tried to keep her composure, but this wasn't something that she could just easily fake the funk about. His heartbeat was steady, and honesty dripped from his words like honey. All Rita wanted was love. That's why she wanted a family. Here was this wolf bearing his soul to her and she was thinking about walking away. How stupid could she be? Her stomach quaked with her pent-up emotions as she began to cry.

"I don't want to be without you either," she cried. "But I-I know you won't be able to accept what I've done."

"How do you know that if you don't tell me, Rita? Just tell me what he did to you. Tell me so I can help you feel empowered again."

"It's not what he did!" She shrieked. "It's what I did! I fucked him Jayce!"

"But if he made you-"

"He didn't make me do anything! I chose to fuck him Jayce! I knew I had a mate, I knew I would be betraying you, and I let him fuck me!" Jayce opened his mouth to speak and then closed it unsure of what he was exactly supposed to say. Rita continued to break down, her shoulders shaking with her cries.

"You tell me I'm a strong woman Jayce, but I didn't fight my way out of Maverick's captivity. I didn't defeat him, I didn't leave him laying in a pool of his own blood. I fucked him! That's why he marked me. That's why he thinks I can lead the she-wolves into his trap. That's how I was able to get Amber, Maya, and Brandy free. He wouldn't have trusted me otherwise! But I should have done something else. I should have fought tooth and nail until I defeated him. Instead I decided to just fuck him. That's who you're trying to mate Jayce. I don't see how you can accept me after what I've done." Unable to handle her shame she covered her face and ran off crying through the tunnels.

Jayce was thrown. Of course, he wasn't happy to hear that Maverick was inside his mate. To know that another wolf had touched what was his. But he also knew that Rita wasn't the type of woman to do something unless it was necessary. And if she hadn't done what she'd did with Maverick, then the pack wouldn't have the plan they did now to take him out. Even if the admission was hard for him to swallow, he wasn't going to make his mate feel any ounce of shame for doing what she had to do to survive. Now was his time to show her that he was going to commit to her no matter the circumstance. Nodding with assurance for himself that he was going to make things right, he followed the sound of Rita's cries all the way to her bedroom. Her door was closed, but he went inside without knocking. She was in bed with her face buried in her pillow crying her eyes out. Jayce stepped inside and closed the door.

"Please just go Jayce," she wept. Jayce ignored her and sat on the edge of the bed. He pulled her up and dragged her across his lap, cradling her like she was a baby. He kissed her forehead.

"Look what you're doing to yourself," he said wiping the tears from her face. He grabbed a spare t-shirt that lay on her bed and held it against her nose.

"Blow," he ordered softly. She blew into the t-shirt while he wiped her nose.

"That's better. Now you don't got snot all over your face." She hiccupped as she looked up at him, curious as to why he wasn't pissed at what she'd done.

"You're not mad?" she squeaked out.

"Mad? Rita, I'm furious." She gasped and tried to move from his lap, but he held her tight. "I'm furious that you think you betrayed me or that I wouldn't want to accept you."

"But-"

"No, but's Rita." She sniffled and continued to gaze at him with her doe-like eyes. "I said what I said about hoping he didn't touch you because I didn't want you to have to live with the fact that he did. And like I said, I'm your mate. Anyone touching you would upset me. But that don't mean I'm gonna love you any less."

"I didn't fight," she whispered. "I should have just kept fighting instead of giving him my body. That doesn't make me strong."

"Fighting comes in many forms, I'm pretty certain of that. But I'm also certain that it was hard as fuck to willingly give your body to someone you despise and pretend you liked it for not only your freedom but the freedom of others. You made a sacrifice other women wouldn't make Rita. That surely sounds like fighting to me. And it sure as hell proves how strong you are."

"You think so?" she asked.

"Yes, baby I do. Not only were you thinking about the young wolves you were thinking about your pack. Because without you giving him your body we wouldn't have the plan we have now to finally get him. We owe a lot to you, Rita."

"I thought about you," she said. "He didn't give me one ounce of pleasure. I didn't want any pleasure from him. But to make it look like he was giving me pleasure I closed my eyes and thought about our first time. How it felt when you touched me. And all the pleasure you gave me. It was the only thing that allowed me not to show my disgust for Maverick."

"Well, I guess that's something. He wasn't better than me was he? Because I swear to god if he was better than me, I'm gonna find one of those wolfs bane guns and shoot myself in the dick." His comment did exactly what he wanted it to. Rita's mouth cured into a shy smile before her body began to shake as she stifled her laughter. But then she let it all out and laughed. Her laughter filled Jayce up, letting him know that he'd done his job.

"If you shoot yourself in the dick what am I supposed to use?"

"You're right," he said smiling. He kissed her on the mouth softly.

"Mate with me," he said softly after a moment of silence. She was smiling but then her smile disappeared.

"We can't," she said.

"Why?"

"If we mate our scents will mix." Rita slapped her forehead upset she hadn't thought of it until then. "If Maverick knows I completed the mated bond with you he'll never believe I'm actually still on his side."

"Shit. You're right. Fuck!" Rita rubbed his face.

"Only a week and then I'm all yours," she said.

"A week is a long ass time," he smiled.

"But I'd wait an eternity to be with you if I have to." Rita snuggled in his arms, pressing her face to his neck devouring herself in his scent. And it was all she and her wolf needed before she conked out for the night.

Chapter Fifteen

Kellan and his wolves watched as their she-wolves fought each other, each viciously and intensely. He knew that the she-wolves were capable of fighting but he was surprised at the level they were on, and in only a week their skills had doubled, even tripled immensely. Gemma was still in short control of her wolf, but was surprisingly beginning to show more and more control. It looked like both her and her wolf liked the idea of kicking ass and that's why they were in sync. Tonight was the night they were going to get Maverick, and Kellan needed to make sure the women were more than ready.

"Stop!" His voice boomed out. The fighting stopped slowly, the she-wolves panting and sweating.

"Good job ladies," he complimented. "I'm satisfied with your fighting skills. Tonight there will be no mercy regarding Maverick or anyone who stands in our way of taking him down. As per the plan, only you women will be entering the club. Rita, you're taking charge of handling Maverick and Bliss I want you to keep the other she-wolves safe until we can get hands on him."

"Don't all rip him to pieces," Kyra said. "Save some for us." Her comment made Kellan think. In some shape or another, Maverick had negatively impacted each one of his she-wolves. And to see them stand there ready to fight was honorable and inspiring.

"It's a deal," Kellan replied. "Everyone go rest up for tonight. Rita and Jayce I need to speak with the both of you." Everyone else left the workout area, Bliss kissed her mate on the cheek before she left the room as well.

"I'm assuming you're going to be my beta couple correct?" Kellan asked.

"Yes," Jayce spoke up

. "We just can't complete the bond because Maverick won't fall for our trap if he knows Rita mated with me."

"Right," Kellan nodded.

"Rita, how strong do you think the other she-wolves are?"

"Is this a trick question?" Rita asked "Like some sort of beta test?" Kellan smiled at her.

"No test. But get used to it. Before I make pack decisions, I consult my beta. The beta is the voice of reasoning and in some cases will keep me from making rash decisions. I'm on the verge of making a decision, but I need to make sure it will be effective. So, how strong you think the she-wolves are?"

"Individually it might be hard to win a fight depending on the strength of the opponent. But I must say when we move as a unit, we're strong. Very strong."

"Jayce you agree?"

"Yeah, I do. Yesterday all of them fucked me, Jaxson, and Tristan up."

"Good," Kellan nodded.

"What decision were you planning on making?" Rita asked.

"You'll see," Kellan responded. "Thanks for your time." His face was straight, but then a smile spread across his lips. Rita made a face as she looked at him. He noticed right away and stopped smiling.

"Sorry," he laughed. "Bliss is being a very naughty wolf in my head right now. And she's projecting very interesting things in my mind. Excuse me." He left the room quickly his arousal very much noticeable. His trail of arousal hung around Rita and Jayce awkwardly. They hadn't touched each other since he'd marked her. They were both sexually frustrated, but Rita hadn't even shown him her naked body with her scars. So staying away from sex was probably a good thing. She knew she couldn't hide it forever but waiting until she was confident enough was key.

"Are you ready for tonight?" Jayce asked her, breaking the silence

"Yes," she replied confidently.

"It's about time we stop living with that creep somewhere out there."

"I'm really upset that we can't mate before this whole ordeal," he admitted.

"I wouldn't want to go into any fight without the strength of my mate."

"I don't want to either," she sighed. Even though she knew it could complicate things both her and her wolf wanted to complete the bond.

"I bet you're wondering why I haven't tried to touch you," he said.

"A little."

"I know I won't have control," he admitted.

"It was hard enough not to complete the bond when I marked you. If I get inside you again, I'll have no control, and I'm going to bite you to bond. There's going to be no stop to that."

"Not if you're not attracted to me anymore," Rita mumbled looking away from him. She knew she should have kept her mouth shut because as a wolf Jayce's hearing was impeccable.

"Why would you say that?" he asked.

"No reason," Rita waved him off. She kissed him on the cheek and tried to just walk away, but Jayce held onto her.

"If there's one thing you ain't gonna do in this relationship Rita, is wave me off and walk away. Don't disrespect me like that." Rita swallowed hard. The look on his face told her that he wasn't messing around.

"I don't know if now is a good time to talk about it. We have to focus on the mission later tonight." Jayce gave her a cold look.

"You know what. Whenever you're ready to stop bullshitting I'll be around." He brushed by her and began walking away.

"Wait!" Rita hurried after him and grabbed his hand. It didn't take anything for him to stop.

"What?"

"I'll tell you what I mean," she said. Even not being ready to come clean about her scars she didn't want him to walk away from her thinking that she was bullshitting him.

"Well...?" Rita shifted on her feet uncomfortably.

"We gotta go to my room," she finally spoke. Jayce moved out of the way so she could walk in front of him leading the way.

"And speaking of your room," Jayce said. "Either you move into my room with me, or I move into your room with you. But I won't sleep separately from you anymore." Rita only nodded. She wouldn't mind sharing the same room with him as long as he was ready to accept the fact that his mate wasn't the same beautiful woman he knew from before.

Reaching her room, she went in first and closed the door once Jayce walked in. He immediately went to the bed where he sat down and kicked off his sneakers. Rita stood in front of him not sure how she was going to approach the situation or how she would even start.

"So what's up?" he asked. Rita didn't know what to say, so she just started undressing. She was wearing a long sleeve workout shirt and leggings. She peeled off her leggings first.

"Wait I told you sex shouldn't be happening between us," Jayce spoke when he felt his mouth start to salivate at her stripping in front of him. But still, she didn't stop stripping. After she pulled down her leggings, she reached for the bottom of her shirt. She took a deep breath before pulling the shirt up and over her head. Jayce gasped at the scars she revealed covering her upper body. There were some on her legs, but he hadn't noticed them until he saw the rest. With her chest rising and falling rapidly she slowly turned in a circle showing him that her scars traveled all around her body. Her back and the backs of her thighs were scarred in a way that looked like thin welts. He knew the only way a wolf ever scarred was a severe injury, or silver. When she made her full circle and faced him again, she wrapped her arms around herself and hung her head low. Though she was scared, Jayce wanted her body more than he wanted anything else.

"Do you remember what I said to you the first time we made love Rita?" he asked her. She didn't look up at him, but she nodded.

"I remember. But we didn't really make love, did we? You sort of fucked me senseless."

"I wanted you that bad." Jayce moved in closer to her and removed her arms from covering herself. He used his index finger, placing it under her chin to lift her head. She locked stares with him.

"You're still the most beautiful wolf I've ever laid my eyes on," Jayce whispered. Rita felt a rush of relief come through her body.

"Scars don't do nothing but tell a story about your sacrifices. I crave you too much to let something as superficial as scars send me running." He placed his hand around the back of her neck and pulled her forward.

"You're still my sexy ass wolf that I plan to fuck all night until the sun rises when we finally complete the bond."

"Only when we complete the bond?" she asked. Jayce smirked at her.

"You're walking a thin line, Rita. I promise." She shrugged and gave him a look that Jayce took as a challenge. He really couldn't have sex with her because there was no way he was going to not bite her. But that didn't mean he couldn't assault her with pleasure. Standing in front of her, Jayce leaned over so he could kiss her deeply. She tried to cover herself again to try to hide her scars, but Jayce took her wrists to keep her from doing so.

"Jayce..." she whispered.

"No hiding," he said sternly.

"Not from your mate." To prove her scars didn't affect him, he bent over and kissed a scar on her chest. She drew in a breath as he continued kissing each and every scar on her upper body. By the time he reached her stomach, she was shaking and breathing heavily. He made her spread her legs. The scent of her arousal invaded his senses. Her honey was dripping down her inner thighs. As he kissed the scars on her thighs, he couldn't help but touch her quivering core. At his touch, Rita jumped, but he calmed her down with another kiss to another scar. Her insides were shaking with anticipation and leaking immensely. He delved a finger into her opening with his middle finger, while his thumb worked on her clit. Her legs trembled, threatening to give out. Before they could give out, Jayce stood and wrapped his arm around her waist. He pecked at her neck then drew his tongue along her chest, creating a trail to her heavy breasts. Without a second thought he pulled her brown nipple into his mouth, moaning at her taste.

"Jayce," she moaned. Jayce held her around the waist with one arm while his other hand was busy pleasuring her womanly core. He walked her towards the bed without looking up from her breast. He only pulled her breast from his mouth so they could fall onto the bed. And when they fell, he removed his finger. She cried out and jacked her hips up not wanting the loss of his finger inside her. Jayce was hard as fuck in his jeans, yearning to make love to his mate but he didn't see how he could do it. To take it off his mind, he slid down her body and spread her legs open. He didn't waste a minute delving into her folds with his tongue. He slurped and sipped at her juices loving the way she tasted. Jayce realized he was about to be feasting all night. He got comfortable on his stomach and continued to suck at her clit. He pushed his tongue down her opening as her first release dribbled out of her.

Rita was seeing stars as even though she came, he was still kissing and sucking at her clit passionately and slowly. His tongue twirled around her clit slowly making her hips jerk before he used the flat of his tongue to lick the underside of her clit. She hardly believed that he was devouring her like this after seeing her scarred body. But his lips was making her orgasm over and over again.

"I don't think I can take it anymore," she cried out as her back bowed. Every time she tried to close her legs, he forced them open and continued to eat her like his last meal. If he didn't stop, surely her clit was going to fall off. Instead of closing her legs, she tried to move back. Seeing what she was doing, he inserted two fingers into her quickly and began jerking them upwards. Rita screamed and closed her eyes as fluids rushed from her insides and squirted back onto Jayce. Her body trembled and convulsed with her large orgasm.

"No more!" she begged as he pinched her clit. Laughing, he stopped touching her and backed away to allow her to recuperate. Licking his lips, he looked down at his handiwork. She was moaning and groaning, rolling all over the bed. Since his t-shirt was soaked, he pulled it over his head and tossed it to the side. He rejoined her in bed, grabbing her up and holding her close to him.

"Damn, you taste good," he spoke. Rita could only respond with a satisfied sigh before digging face into his chest. She was asleep in no time.

Chapter Sixteen

Rita awoke later that night alone in her room. Jayce's scent was still fresh on her sheets and left a trail to the door, so she knew he probably had recently gotten up as well. She looked out of the window created through the rock in her room and saw the brightness of the moon. It was time to get down to business. Getting out of bed, she went to wash up before dressing in the sexy leather outfit the she-wolves had decided they were going to wear. It was funny because she was completely iffy about wearing the short skirt and halter top because of her scars, but now, for some reason, she just felt rejuvenated. She felt like she was a badass shifter ready to hunt and kill. That's how she wanted to feel, not like some type of victim. Even though she did go through something traumatizing, she was going to uplift herself.

Dressed and ready for their mission, Rita left her bedroom and went through the tunnels to the kitchen. The scents of her pack mates greeted her when she emerged from the tunnels. The she-wolves were all dressed in similar leather outfits, and the men were all only wearing sweatpants. They were munching on sandwiches.

275

"Sorry, I'm late to the party," Rita said joining them. Jayce handed her a sandwich.

"You're not late," he said kissing her on the cheek. For a moment, Rita felt self-conscious because everyone was looking at her and no doubt seeing her body was littered with scars, but it was Bliss who broke the silence.

"Rita, you look amazing," she said, boosting Rita's confidence.

"Jayce, you're a lucky guy."

"Hell, I'd hit it," Jaxson said. Jayce barred his teeth at Jaxson and growled. Jaxson laughed and backed up.

"You always fuckin' with me." Jayce snapped at him.

"Calm down, fellas. Let's leave that energy for later," Kellan said with a smirk, but then he looked at Rita.

"Jaxson is right though." Not only did Jayce growl at him but so did Bliss. She snapped out her claws.

"Tryna lose your dick?" she asked him darkly. Rolling his eyes, Kellan simply grabbed Bliss by the back of the neck and rubbed the sides of her neck, and she calmed down instantly. He winked at Rita making her smile.

"You know, Rita, if you want some girl on girl action, then I can agree with both Kellan and Jaxson. I'd hit it too." Kyra added in. That had everyone gasping while Rita laughed.

"Hey, she-wolf or not, I'll still fight you for coming at my mate," Jayce said.

"Back up."

"Oh, relax! Your mate is sexy as fuck, take pride in it. Shit, every female in the Phoenix pack is sexy as fuck. I mean, even Mira is cute and all." Mira smiled and nodded at the compliment. She was dressed similarly to the other she-wolves, but her and Dell and the other wolves in his pack were quiet. Maya, Brandy, and Amber were set to stay back in the cave. Kellan thought they were too young to witness anything that would happen that night.

"Enough of this," Jayce said waving his hands around.

"Let's go! We got a shifter to find and rip to pieces."

"Let's go." Kellan clapped. They all headed towards the exit of the cave, but Jayce grabbed Rita and held her protectively.

"You keep away from my mate with your little horny bi-curious ass," Jayce said to Kyra pushing her away from them. Kyra laughed and slapped his hand off her. She was going to say something, but she felt Jaxson's eyes on her, and certainly when she looked at him, he was glaring at her. Submitting, she put her hands up and let it go. Jaxson nodded in approval before giving her another last heated stare and walking by her.

Staying in human form, the Phoenix pack traveled the woods swiftly, moving with agility only their kind was equipped with. They ran through the woods without breaking a sweat until they finally reached the edge of the woods. Once there, the males stopped.

"We'll be waiting right here," Kellan said to them.

"It's close enough to speak into our minds should you need to."

"We got this, ladies," Bliss said.

"Let's go get that asshole." Before they left off, Bliss and Rita gave their mates kisses. Gemma looked awkwardly at Tristan, and she was ready to walk away, but then something made her stop. She looked back at Tristan with her arms crossed.

"Kiss your mate so they can go." Kellan ordered him. He grunted and went over to Gemma, placing a hard kiss on her lips.

"Please be safe, Gemma," he said softly. She nodded at him before backing away and going towards the other she-wolves. Then they were off, moving towards the town that lay just up ahead.

It was a Saturday night, so the town was anything but quiet. When the she-wolves made it to the streets, they began attracting jealous stares from women and longing stares from men. Maverick's nightclub wasn't too far from the spot in the woods where the males were waiting. Rita could smell both humans and shifters the moment they entered the club. She figured Maverick would play to both crowds, but she didn't think the humans suspected they were partying with wolf shifters and other animal shifters. The club was dark, but their heightened senses allowed them to see perfectly. Human girls were dancing on the stage, and some were dancing for money on men on the dancefloor. The place was packed, and men saw a group of new women who they wanted to hump and dance on. She had to force herself not to growl and snap her canines at the unwanted humping.

Stay here, I'll go find him. Rita spoke in the minds of the she-wolves. They nodded as she walked away to find Maverick. She didn't get far before a hand grabbed hold of her. Turning around, it was Rory. He didn't say a word as he began leading her somewhere. They walked up a flight of spiral stairs in the corner of the club that led to an office. Maverick was leaning back in the office chair but popped up when Rory and Rita entered.

"Rita." He gasped.

"You actually came back. I thought I was just going to have to find you and kill you."

"Yeah, well I'm here now, and so are the other she-wolves." Maverick inhaled and sniffed making his nose twitch.

"You smell like Jayce." He accused.

"If I didn't let him mark me, he would be suspicious, so I let him mark me to believe I was going to mate with him," she said.

"Good work." Maverick smiled.

"About the she-wolves, I told them we would stay here for a bit, but they want to go back to the woods. Bliss is getting antsy, and if we stay much longer, the whole plan will fall apart, and I don't think you can even snatch them up in here. The place is too damn crowded."

"Alright, take them back to the woods. I'll follow close behind, but I need proof you brought them."

"Come look," Rita stated. She looked over at Hera who was still wearing silver cuffs. She stood when Maverick did, ready to follow him out. Rita knew Hera didn't trust her, but Rita didn't care. She had Maverick eating out of her hand, and that's all that mattered. He left the office and looked down into the crowd of writhing bodies. Sure enough, the females of the Phoenix pack were loitering around waiting for Rita to return.

"How'd you get the males not to come?"

"Told them it was a woman's night out. They didn't suspect a thing, but Bliss mated with Kellan. If she gets any more antsy, Kellan is going to feel it and come snooping to make sure she's okay. That's why we gotta get back to the woods where she's comfortable and won't alert Kellan. Give me three bottles of champagne to take back to the woods so I can make sure no one wants to go home just yet." Maverick went back into his office and retrieved the bottles of champagne from a cabinet.

"Here. Go on and get out of here. Rory, Levi, and I will be following."

"Good." Rita tried to leave, but before he let her go, he pulled her arm bringing her back to him. He placed a kiss on her lips, and Rita fought hard not to cringe.

"Save it for the victory, baby," she said to him pulling away. He smiled at her as he watched her walk away.

Rita hurried back to the other wolves with the champagne. That was the sign that everything was going according to plan. That way they didn't have to speak about it and Maverick possibly hear. If she didn't have the champagne, then that would have meant something went wrong, but everything was going to plan. They left the club promptly. Kyra took one of the bottles and popped it open and began to guzzle the champagne straight from the bottle. They laughed and talked about miscellaneous shit as a way to let Maverick believe they weren't suspicious about Rita's plan.

In the woods where they had left the males, the area was clear like planned. Rita popped the other bottles of champagne and sprayed it on the other she-wolves to help mask the scent of the rest of the pack from Maverick.

"Looks like fun." Maverick spoke appearing at the edge of the woods with Hera next to him. The women gasped and backed up holding onto each other.

"Don't even think about running." Maverick ordered. Levi and Rory appeared then, circling around them.

"Good job, Rita. Just like we planned." Rita left the females and went to stand next to Maverick.

"Rita?" Bliss gasped. "You-you set us up?"

"How could you do that?" Kyra exclaimed.

"Because I wanted to." Rita snapped.

"I was supposed to be the Alpha female, Bliss, then you came and ruined that for me, but now, me and Maverick have a plan where we both can be the Alphas we want to. I suggest you don't fight him, Bliss."

"You bitch." Bliss gritted.

"Damn," Maverick said licking his lips.

"I can already see myself fucking each and every one of you." He pointed at Gemma. "I smell your cherry." He growled.

"Pig." She snapped at him.

"You'll be calling me daddy soon enough. Time to go, ladies." Right on time, Kellan, Jayce, Tristan, Jaxson, Dell, and his wolves dropped from the treetops. Jaxson and Tristan dropped directly behind Levi and Rory. At the same time, Tristan and Jaxson held Levi and Rory by the necks and twisted hard, snapping their heads from their bodies. They ripped Levi and Rory's heads clean off. Maverick stood there in shock unable to move. Rita backed away from him joining the other she-wolves as the males faced off with Maverick.

"You sly bitch." Maverick growled at Rita. Rita only smiled.

"Funny what pussy can make a man believe," she said.

"I told you she was gonna double cross you." Hera snapped. Maverick ignored her. Hera stepped up like she was going to start fighting, but Mira stepped up too.

"Try something. I dare you." She growled. Even though she had caused drama in the pack last week, she'd been on her best behavior, and she was effective in having Hera stuck in her tracks afraid to attack.

"Why don't we just fight it out. You and me. Winner gets the pack," Maverick said to Kellan.

"Nah, this ain't that kind of fight," Kellan replied.

"So, you and your wolves gonna jump me, huh?" Maverick asked.

"Well, me and my male wolves ain't gonna do nothin' to ya'. My female wolves though? That's a different story." Kellan and the other men backed away, leaving the females front and center. In that moment, the women understood that Kellan was giving them power by allowing them to take down the man that terrorized each of them in some way, shape, or form. Kellan hadn't told the women what he wanted them to do, and surprisingly, none of the women looked worried. They all smiled at Kellan before turning and grilling Maverick with death in their eyes. Even Gemma whipped out her claws ready to fight, and in that moment, where all the men were standing behind the women, Kellan felt a sense of pride. The she-wolves in his pack were fierce, and he learned that he didn't have to baby them or keep them hidden in safety. They were capable of defending the pack too.

"Wait, you aren't serious, are you?" Maverick asked laughing. He bent over slapping his knee like he was watching a comedy show. Kyra tilted her head to the side watching as he was laughing. Remembering how he tried to ruin her chances of ever having pups anger filled through her. She'd never forget how he'd attack her. So while he was busy laughing his ass off Kyra marched up to him with her claws drawn. When she got close, he stood straight and looked down at her. Kyra swung, connecting her claws to his face. On impact of her hand to his face, she raised her leg and kicked him hard in the stomach knocking the air out of him. He fell to the ground with his cheek bleeding and holding his stomach. He looked at Kyra all sense of humor gone from his face. He went to launch himself at Kyra but the other she-wolves were quicker. While he was down, they all ran forward claws and teeth ready for the attack. As a unit, they attacked him at once striking with blows they knew would keep him crippled. But he knew he was getting his ass kicked in human form. He pushed the women back, and in a thrust of power and in under a minute he was a large wolf standing over them. Gemma shifted just as quickly and was the first to launch herself at Maverick's big wolf. The other she-wolves followed suit.

Even though Maverick was larger the she-wolves were stronger as a pack. And even though Maverick was biting through their flesh and dragging his claws through their them not one of the she-wolves showed any weakness. To finally get him down, Rita pounced on top of Maverick and clamped her jaws around his shoulder and neck. Gemma and Kyra clawed at his hind legs, while Bliss punctured his ribs. Not being able to stand or breathe sent him down immediately. Rita ripped out a large chunk of his flesh from his neck. The power of his wolf dimmed, and he shifted back to his human form. Blood poured from every crevice of his body. The she-wolves backed off and shifted into their human forms. Dell's wolves were carrying bags with tunics. They quickly dressed in the tunics, so they weren't walking around naked.

"Great, a bunch of women beat me up. Happy?" Maverick growled. Rita stepped in his face, crushing his nose.

"Shut the fuck up," She spat. Gripping onto his arm, she twisted it with all the strength she could muster and yanked it out of its socket. He howled in pain and writhed on the ground as she did the same thing to his other arm.

"Help me, you bitch!" Maverick shouted at Hera. But Hera was looking at the scene in horror. Without a second thought, she backed away into the woods then she was running off not wanting any part of what was happening.

"So much for alpha female," Rita joked. Maverick closed his eyes and tried to shift back into his wolf but with broken limbs that wasn't going to happen.

"Just let me go. I won't bother your pack again."

"Funny you should ask to be let go," Bliss spoke up.

"I begged you time and time again to just let me leave our relationship but each time to beat me down until I couldn't even get up to walk. And then what'd you do when I nearly got free from your psycho ass? You drove your claws through my stomach and threw me into the woods to bleed out to death." Bliss showed him her claws.

"Too bad for you Kellan found me where you dumped my body huh," Bliss said. She kneeled down and jabbed her claws into his stomach. Kyra came over and stood over him.

"You nearly ripped my uterus to shreds because you were forcing me to have a pup with you," she said squatting down above his bare hips. She grabbed hold of his dick.

"NO! NO! DON'T!" He screamed. But Kyra showed him no mercy. She dug her claws around the flesh of his dick and shredded it until blood coated her fingers. Unable to do what she wanted as a human, she took off her tunic and shifted into her wolf. With the power and strength of her animal, she locked her jaw around Maverick dick and yanked, biting it clean off. Her wolf tossed his dismembered organ to the ground while blood spurted everywhere. Even if this would kill a human, it wouldn't kill a wolf. And that's what made it torture. Just like he'd tortured all of them.

Gemma picked up his dick. Maverick was screaming his head off, so Gemma stuffed his dick into his mouth, shoving it deep into his throat until he began to choke. Because they didn't know how else to end it in their human forms, they pulled the tunics over their heads and shifted again. Maverick watched, with his dick stuck in his throat as the she-wolves gathered around him. They were growling menacingly over him. There were no need for any more words. He saw what his fate was going to be. They simply had no mercy. All at once, the she-wolves pounced onto his mangled body and began ripping and clawing him to pieces. Their jaws chewed through his bone leaving nothing to be salvaged. When his life force left his body, the she-wolves backed off, panting heavily. They shifted back to human form in a rush of shifting bones and power. Once they were all human, they looked at the mangled remains of Maverick. He looked like raw ground meat, and it didn't gross them out. In fact, all of them had tears in their eyes. Not because they were sad, but because they were rejuvenated and took back something they didn't think was possibly.

"He's gone," Bliss gasped. She looked at her sisters before jumping up and down.

"We fucking killed his ass!" she cheered. Looking back at the men, they were staring at them with their mouths open.

"What?" Rita asked dressing back in the tunic.

"This was the plan," she said.

"Well we knew we were gonna torture his ass this way," Kellan said.

"But seeing y'all do this put fear in my damn heart. And Gemma?!" Kellan shook his head and rubbed his throat.

"The dick part was brutal!"

"Kyra was the one who ripped the shit off," Gemma laughed.

"But that's what he gets for messing with the Phoenix pack females." Tristan was full of pride at the way his mate handled the torture of Maverick. Any other young wolf would have run. But no, she fought.

"Let's head back to the cave," Kellan said.

"Maya, Amber, and Brandy are probably sick with anticipation with when we're coming back."

"Yes and I have a wolf to mate," Jayce said looking at Rita.

"Me and Tristan will stay back to burn the rest of Maverick's body," Jaxson said.

"We'll see everyone back at the cave."

"Wait!" Mira spoke up suddenly. She looked around the dark woods on high alert.

"What?" Kellan asked.

"There's someone out there," she whispered. None of the other wolves had sensed someone in their presence. But they all knew that Mira was more than just a normal shifter. Kellan didn't sense a presence of anyone, but he heard the shift of the air and then arrows were being shot at them in rapid succession.

"EVERYONE GET DOWN!" Kellan boomed. But as he said that, he felt pain within the bonds he had with his pack. Tristan was hovering over Gemma to protect her, but she'd already been hit. So had Jayce and Jaxson.

"Bliss move!" Rita screamed. Bliss was trying to run towards Kellan when Rita had screamed. Bliss stopped in her tracks trying to look for the source of the attack. Rita ran towards Bliss and pushed her out of the way of an oncoming arrow. Kellan screamed in pain as he felt something pierce his heart. He touched his chest, but he had no wound. Which meant he was feeling his pack's pain. The whirring sounds of arrows stopped immediately making the area around them deathly quiet. Kellan fell to his knees as his heart constricted.

"Bliss?" Kellan gasped, fearful it was his mate who was hurt. Bliss was on the ground, but then she slowly got up. Kellan looked next to her. Rita was struggling to breathe as an arrow stuck out of the middle of her chest.

"No, no, no," Jayce scrambled over to where Rita lay. He scooped her up in his arms. She began coughing up blood as she tried to speak.

"I got you," Jayce said. He held the end of the arrow and quickly pulled it from her chest. Rita squealed in pain and coughed up more blood. Jayce assumed she'd be able to heal if she shifted, but then he looked at the arrow. The tips were silver. His heart crushed.

"No," he wept. Shot straight through the heart with silver was a death sentence. Every shifter knew that.

"It's okay," she gasped out spitting blood from her mouth. She held onto his hand tightly.

"No, it's not," Jayce said.

"What am I supposed to do without you?" he asked.

"Live," she breathed.

"Please-I want you to-be happy."

"I can't," he exclaimed shaking his head wildly. But Rita only smiled at him through her pain. She made a suffocated sound before the hand that was holding his loosened. Her eyes closed and her body sank giving out its last breath before going limp.

"Rita, Rita baby please." Jayce shook her trying to wake her up, but his ears didn't pick up a heartbeat. She was gone. Letting out a large sob he pressed her chest to his face and cried heavily. His heart, his soul, his very life force felt like it was being crushed into non-existence. She'd asked him to be happy, but she didn't know she took his happiness with her when she took her last breath. And then his life was over just as much as hers was.

****

Dell stared down at the dark cloaked figure he and his wolves had caught trying to run away. He had a pouch filled with wolfsbane and silver tipped arrows.

"I told Kellan you got away. I held up my part of the deal now hold up yours." The stranger looked at Dell.

"I just want power," he replied. "So I'm attacking a powerful pack."

"You don't smell like a shifter," Dell commented.

"Hell, you have no smell at all." The stranger's hooded cloak covered his face, and Dell saw nothing but teeth.

"Who said I was a shifter?" the stranger asked.

"I'm gonna let you go and not tell Kellan about this," Dell said.

"But you have to allow me access to these weapons you have. My pack will need further protection, and I like the looks of these weapons." Dell was speaking the truth. His pack was going to need more protection. But there was more he didn't say aloud. He just knew that this stranger would introduce him to weapons that would make him stronger. Perhaps even stronger than Kellan.

The stranger rattled off sparse directions to a section of the woods. Dell had never been there, but he could follow directions very well.

"That's where you'll find me," he grunted.

"Always come alone." The stranger turned and walked off then leaving Dell and his wolves.

"Let's go," Dell said. They shifted altogether and ran in the direction of Kellan's cave not even noticing that Hera was hiding in a treetop listening to their whole conversation.

****

Jayce's agonizing cries rumbled through the silence of the woods around them. Each she-wolf had tears flooding their eyes. Bliss was holding onto Kellan crying softly while Kyra held onto Jaxson and Gemma was holding onto Tristan. Dell had run off to try and find whoever was shooting the arrows in the first place with his pack. They hadn't returned yet. Kellan kissed Bliss on the forehead before leaving her to go over to Jayce. He tried to take Rita from Jayce's arms, but Jayce snapped at him and pushed Kellan's hand away.

"Don't fucking touch her!" he cried.

"Jayce you have to let her go," Kellan said. "She's gone."

"I hope you're fucking grateful," Jayce spat at him. "She took the arrow meant for your mate."

"I know that Jayce," Kellan whispered. Kellan didn't even know what to say. His best friend had lost his mate because she'd saved Kellan's mate.

"I'm so sorry," Jayce whispered to Rita's corpse. "I was supposed to protect you." Kellan rubbed Jayce's back not even sure how else to comfort his friend. The she-wolves quickly gathered around Jayce and tried to comfort him in the same way. Mira was the last of the she-wolves to come over.

"Give her to me," she said to Jayce. Jayce looked at her with bloodshot eyes.

"No," he strained out not wanting to let Rita go.

"Come on Jayce, let her go," Jaxson coaxed softly. They knew Jayce wasn't going to willingly let her go, so the she-wolves began taking Rita's limp body from Jayce while the men pried Jayce's arms from around her. Jayce began crying harder at having Rita taken from his hold. Kellan held him back as the women set Rita in front of Mira. Mira ran her hands up and down Rita's body.

"What are you doing?!" Jayce shrieked. But Mira ignored him. She began chanting in a native language. First, it was just whispers, but then her voice began to slowly rise. Her eyes, chest, and hands began glowing like the color of the moonlight.

"What in the…" Kellan was speechless and had no idea what the fuck Mira was doing. He didn't know if he should stop her or not.

Mira placed one hand on Rita's forehead and her other hand on Rita's chest right over her wound. She began chanting louder her voice becoming deeper and deeper as if she was being taken over by another entity. Her glowing eyes looked down at Rita, and she began to jerk her hands like she was giving Rita CPR. Then she looked up to the sky, bellowing that chant in her deep voice. Lightning struck around them that emanated from Mira's glowing body. She screamed as her body went into some sort of shock. Energy was zapped out of the atmosphere for only a second in which Rita's body jumped. Mira stopped glowing and fell away weakly. Rita's eyes popped open, and she drew in a deep breath as she arched off the ground. She fell back down to the ground limply and her eyes closed, but her chest rose and fell with her breathing. Kellan felt an ignite of a pulse inside him and his body was filled with Rita's essence, and his ears rang with the sound of her heartbeat. He looked at Jayce who was sitting there, shock filling his features. He wiped the stained tears from his face. Mira sat up slowly, still weak.

"Hurry. You need to complete your mating bond so she can share your strength. It'll help her." Jayce was confused, but he crawled over to his mate. Her eyes were closed, but her chest was rising and falling. Her wound had closed, but she was still scarred. Jayce looked up at Mira.

"Go! You don't give her strength she's gonna die again!" Jayce realized Mira had given him a second chance.

"I-"

"Just go! Thank me later!" Mira winced in her own pain. Jayce scooped Rita up in his arms and was dashing through the woods to get back to their cave.

"You can heal people?" Kellan asked Mira.

"When I was a baby my tribe performed a ritual that gave me the ability to heal. But it can only work if the person is deserving of life. Much like the wolf bite. You can only be granted the gift of a shifter if the universe deems you worthy of it. So the universe has deemed Rita was well worth living again. Only downside is that I get weakened by the ritual. I won't be able to regain my strength until the full moon again. I won't be able to travel with Dell and the pack."

"Don't worry about that. What you have done is a debt we have to repay you for. You can stay with my pack under our protection for as long as you need to recover," Kellan said. Bliss came over to Mira.

"I know we have had our troubles," Bliss said.

"But you didn't have to do this, and you did. Thank you. Rita is more than just our packmate."

"I screwed things up by opening my mouth. This is my way of showing that I can be useful to the pack in more than just causing drama." Bliss nodded at her.

"I'll take her back to the cave," Jaxson said coming over to them. He scooped Mira in her arms ready to carry her off.

"Gemma and Kyra go with him. Keep him protected in case whoever was shooting at us comes back. It'll be harder for Jaxson to defend himself while carrying Mira back," Kellan said. Without question, Gemma and Kyra went off with Jaxson. Both she-wolves were bleeding from wounds of the arrows, but none of the wounds were life-threatening.

Tristan, Bliss, and Kellan were the last ones left. While Bliss watched, Kellan and Tristan created a fire to burn Maverick's body. In the process of burning the body, Dell reached out to Kellan in his mind.

We lost the trail. But we're going to do a perimeter to make sure there's no lurkers around, Dell spoke.

Good. You can meet us back at the cave and update me when you're done. Kellan looked at Tristan and Bliss.

"Let's go home. Dell will meet us there." Tristan put out the fire on Maverick's body when his bones disintegrated to make sure nothing else in the woods caught fire. Knowing Bliss was weakened after the fight with Maverick, Kellan bent down so Bliss could climb onto his back and they could hurry back to the safety of their home

Chapter Seventeen

Jayce placed Rita on his bed softly and quickly undressed her. Her heart was still beating, but as each minute passed, it got slower and slower. Jayce undressed and got into the bed next to her.

"Rita, baby, open your eyes and look at me." Her eyes opened only slightly. Jayce didn't know if they could even complete the bond without sex, but he was going to try. Knowing the most sensitive place to put his bite was on her inner thigh near her womanly core. Jayce got between her legs and opened them wide so he could bite down. Focusing on that magic link inside them that made them mates, Jayce let his wolf teeth fall from his gums and pierce Rita's sensitive flesh. He felt the power of the bond begin to knit together slowly. Closing his eyes, he let the memories of Rita's laughter, her attitude, and the way she loved him fuel the bond giving it power to knit together faster. He thought about how he was going to fill her belly with as many pups as he could, how he was going to give every bit of himself to love her and appreciate her life.

Rita felt a swelling in her body whereas before she just felt gelatinous. Now she was being filled with a sense of power that began to overwhelm her. She felt the enormity of Jayce's love for her. Behind her eyes, she saw flashes of his memories of their times together and what he loved most about her. She even saw another projection of her carrying a belly ripe with his pup. Her hormones came raging to life, spurting arousal from her pussy. Her body registered his bite, and when her eyes opened, they were glowing with the power of her wolf. Her body jerked off the bed as his bite sent her over the edge causing her to orgasm without him having to even touch her intimately. She screamed as her spirit latched itself back to her body, and the mating bond was halfway knit together. The moment Jayce let go of her thigh, Rita popped up. She sat on his lap, wrapping her legs around his waist. He titled his head to the side giving her access to the side of his neck and shoulder. She wasted no time biting down hard on his shoulder. Jayce jerked as the mating bond sealed together. All at once, the both of them were enveloped in each other's essence. They could feel each other's wants and desires and their life forces. Jayce was racked with sobs at feeling his mate alive and within him when just moments ago he was holding her limp body in his arms. Rita felt his sorrow. She let her teeth recede and looked into his eyes before she kissed him deeply, pushing her tongue into his mouth trying to savor the taste of her mate.

I'm alive, baby. Don't cry anymore, she said into his mind. She raised her hips and aligned herself with his arousal before sinking down on his length. He hissed in pleasure and guided her hips up and down his shaft. Her muscles clamped around his shaft as pleasure took hold of her. Jayce was so wound up he couldn't control himself. He rose up on his knees, holding her under her bottom, so she didn't fall off his shaft. He switched their positions, making them fall onto the bed with her under him. He held her legs open at the crook of his elbows and continued stroking her deeply. She used her claws and marked him up and down his back, and Jayce didn't even care. He pushed her over the edge, fucking her as deeply as he possibly could.

He'd lost her. She had died in his arms. And the fact that he could do this with her now made him want to give her his all. He wanted to make love to her until he was physically weak. He pressed her legs against her chest until her knees were touching her ears. Her cries of ecstasy filled their large room in the luxury cave. He felt her pleasure through their pulsing mating bond. It allowed for him to know just when she was hitting her peak.

Pressing her further into a ball; his hips slammed against her and he continued to thrust powerfully. Her walls were gushing and making slurping sounds to the beat of his strokes.

"Fuck Jayce! I'm coming," she screamed. Jayce let out a string of his own curses as her walls gripped him tight in her orgasm. Feeling her pleasure plus his own pleasure nearly made him pop like a balloon, but he pulled out of her quickly to save himself. Her legs flopped down as her chest rose up and down slowly.

"Rita," he called her name fiercely. She picked up her head and locked eyes with him. He felt like it was too good to be true. Like he was delirious and his mate wasn't laying in front of him; exhausted from an orgasm. But she looked into his eyes. Their bond made both of their eyes glow. He crawled up her body never averting his eyes. She didn't break eye contact either as slowly rested her head back the closer up her body he got. When he hovered above her; he pressed his arousal to her opening and slipped inside of her.

"I'll never live without you Rita," he breathed as he stroked her slowly.

"You die. And I die." She gasped and clawed his back as he surged deeper into her channel.

"You're mine. Forever," he growled.

"Forever," she whispered as her body trembled as tiny orgasms tingled through her.

"You feel so fucking good," he whimpered almost on the verge of tears. Completing the bond with your mate brought forth so many emotions Jayce felt like he was about to erupt. To fell her essence completely and to be giving her his essence was indescribable.

"Come for me," she gasped out. Jayce shook his head violently.

"No. I don't want this to ever end." And that was true. Not after almost losing her the way he did. He wanted this moment to last forever. Using her strength; Rita pushed them over. Jayce allowed for her to get on top. He held her at the hips as she began grinding on his engorged shaft.

"I'm here now," she breathed as she rocked her hips. Planting her hands flat against his chest; she began to bounce hard on his shaft loving the way he glided in and out of her.

"You don't have to hold it," she moaned. "I'll always be here Jayce. I won't ever leave you." Jayce's stomach clenched.

"No I have to hold it," he gritted. Rita grabbed him under the chin and squeezed his cheeks together. She glared harder into his eyes.

"Give in to my love Jayce. And I promise I'll be your mate forever. We'll grow old together." Jayce turned them onto their side in a fast motion. He tongued her down as he drew her close to his body and hooked her top leg over the crook in his elbow.

"Forever?" He asked as if he didn't believe her. His hips grinded against her as he stroked her deeply.

"Forever," she breathed in confirmation. She lifted her head giving him her neck. He embedded his teeth into her soft flesh; moaning as his strokes sped up. Unable to hold it and believing her words; Jayce finally let go. His back bowed, his toes curled, and his body trembled as he released himself deep inside her. She cried out in pleasure as his orgasm triggered another one of hers, his bite amplifying her pleasure.

For a moment the both of them lay still; just breathing through their passion. Jayce unlatched his teeth from her neck and licked the bite.

"You thought you were gonna be fucking me all night?" she asked. "Are you crazy?!" Rita asked. Immediately Jayce had to laugh. His mate was alive. Jayce cracked a smile as he looked at her beautiful face.

"Do you smell that?" he asked. She took a deep breath, inhaling. A large smile came over her face.

"Our scents mixed together," she replied. Jayce rested his forehead against hers.

"How did I come back?" Rita asked. "It was silver."

"Mira. She did some tribal native type shit." Rita moved her head so she could look at the scar on her chest.

"Another scar." She sighed. "But I'd rather be scarred for life if I could get to spend that life with you." Jayce kissed her on the lips. Now they were officially mated, and the both of them felt within each other that they were ready to start their lives together as a mated couple.

****

Bliss was pacing the kitchen while everyone was sitting and eating. She didn't have an appetite. She was worried about Rita. She felt Rita's pulse, but she didn't know if what Mira did would make Rita a killer zombie or make Rita crazy because she didn't understand why she was pulled from the afterlife. Even though she was weak, Mira was waiting in the kitchen with them to hear if Rita would be alright. From the tunnels, Bliss heard Jayce speaking softly to someone, and then both Rita and Jayce emerged from the tunnels. Their mixed scent bloomed like a flower in Bliss' nose. Bliss sighed the hardest she'd ever sighed and ran over to Rita hugging her tightly.

"Oh, my God." she breathed.

"Thank goodness you're alright." Rita chuckled.

"Thanks, Bliss." Everyone came up to hug Rita and Jayce congratulating them on their mating. Once that was done, Rita went over to Mira. She bowed down as a show of respect.

"Thank you, Mira," she said. Mira bowed as well showing Rita the same respect.

"Does anyone know who was shooting at us?" Jayce asked.

"Dell wasn't able to find them," Kellan replied.

"Well, we need to-" Bliss was cut off by a searing of pain through her abdomen. Her eyes went wide. She looked at Mira who smiled and nodded at her.

"Told you," Mira said.

"Oh, no," Bliss moaned. She doubled over as her heating cycle began. All the male wolves jumped to attention as the force of her arousal hit them hard. Kellan grabbed her up by the waist and ran off with her through the tunnels to their room. The moment she was gone, the waves of arousal disappeared.

"Looks like the cave walls are thick enough to block the effects of the heating cycle," Jayce commented.

"Thankfully," Tristan mumbled. He glanced at Gemma before looking away. Gemma just shook her head and looked at Rita.

"I hope she gets pregnant," Gemma said.

"I know you wants pups." She looked at Rita.

"Yeah, I do, but there's no rush. I am after all the Beta female. I need to be around to help this guy out," Rita said poking Jayce with her elbow. Jayce smiled and slung his arm around her shoulder before leading her out of the kitchen and back towards their bedroom. Jaxson scooped Mira up from the chair, and Kyra followed him to take Mira back to her room to rest.

That left Tristan and Gemma alone. They looked at each other for a long while. Gemma wanted nothing but to crawl up his body and position herself over his length and ride him while he was standing.

"We have to mate each other, you know that right?" she asked. "I don't know about you, but I don't want to be in pain."

"Don't worry about it," he replied smoothly. Dell and his wolves came into the kitchen ending Gemma's alone time with her mate. Dell looked at her and smiled, while one of his wolves did the same. Gemma smiled at the submissive wolf before she left the kitchen. Tristan noticed the interaction between them and didn't say a word, but he was going to keep his eye on it. Tristan walked by the wolf making sure to bump into him for intimidation before he continued to get to the cellar so he could work out.

Once Tristan was gone, Dell snapped his jaws at his wolf. He growled in his anger.

"What in the fuck were you looking at Gemma like that for?" Dell growled at him.

"What you think?" Niles replied. "She's a gorgeous wolf, and my wolf likes her."

"Yeah, well, she's off limits."

"Why? 'Cause Tristan?"

"He'll kill you," Dell stated.

"I'll take my chances." Niles shrugged.

"Gemma is almost worth dying for. Besides, it won't take much to get her seen as her own damn mate don't want her."

****

Hera followed the cloaked stranger to a small hut clear across the woods. It wasn't a well-traveled place in the woods and seemingly perfect for someone who wanted to hide. The moment the stranger pulled his cloak from over his head, Hera dropped down from the trees.

"Don't move." She ordered. The stranger stood frozen.

"I saw what you did to Kellan and his pack and the conversation you had with Dell."

"You always seemed so smart, Hera," he said. Hera nearly jumped.

"How the hell you know my name?" she asked.

"Because I studied every and anything regarding wolves and their packs. Because I wanted it so bad."

"Turn around." Hera ordered. But he didn't.

"Hera, do you want to join me? Do you want power? Do you want to take back what others have ripped from you?"

"Yes…" Hera responded slowly.

"I think we have a great need for each other," he said.

"And I believe this is the universe's way of bringing us together." Slowly, he turned around. Hera fought the scream that came out of her mouth when she saw his mangled features. He was scarred horribly and looked like his face was going to fall off his bones. Through the severity of his features, Hera recognized the man.

"You're-you're Bliss's father." Hera gasped. "Bryce."

"Yes. Maverick promised me something and deceived me. Unfortunately, the Phoenix pack killed him before I could. Bliss was given the power of something I wanted badly while I was left like this, and I plan on making her life and that of her pack a living hell." He held his hand out.

"Come. There is a lot for us to learn. A lot for us to plan. I'm sure you want a front row seat to the demise of the Phoenix pack." Hera looked at his outstretched hand for a moment before she took it. He smiled at her through his torn up face and laughed manically.

To be continued...

CPSIA information can be obtained
at www.ICGtesting.com
Printed in the USA
LVHW012028051218
599379LV00001B/83/P

9 781790 436040